ROGUES
TO
REMEMBER

ROGUES
TO
REMEMBER

A SHORT STORY ANTHOLOGY BY

BILL LEE

GLB Publishers, San Francisco   First Edition

Published in the United States by
GLB Publishers
P.O. Box 78212, San Francisco, CA 94107 USA

Number 1 of ROGUES Series

Cover Design by Timothy Lewis and W.L. Warner

ISBN 1-879194-00-7

First printing, February, 1991
Reprinted 1992
10 9 8 7 6 5 4 3 2

FOREWORD BY THE AUTHOR

The stories included here are explicit gay male action, and make no pretense at teaching or endorsing any particular activity. It is recognized that many of the scenes include activities that are risky in the age of AIDS with unfamiliar partners. The author believes that fiction can be used as a substitute for risk-taking; if these pages become sticky, they may have succeeded in preventing transmission of the AIDS virus.

The last two segments of this volume are examples of fiction writing for the purpose of educating and promoting safer sex.

Names, characters, places, and incidents are either the products of the author's imagination or are used fictitiously, and any resemblance to actual persons, living or dead, events, or locales is entirely coincidental.

This book was inspired by maleness and all that encompasses. I hope other males like it.

TABLE OF CONTENTS

NEVER THE SAME AGAIN

Carl and John had attended Marine basic together, suffered under the same Drill Sergeant, sweated together in calisthenics, and gone to the same school for Military Police. They were buddies, *Semper Fi* and all that crap. So it was only natural that they double-dated when they had the same liberty weekends in San Diego.

They had met two girls the previous weekend in a bar and made a date for this particular night, expecting them to be pushovers. They rented a double room in a cheap hotel on Main Street. It wouldn't be the first time they had screwed broads in the same room, and watched each other while they were doing it. They were buddies, right? Sometimes they even timed their strokes to coincide, and unconsciously tried to cum at the same time.

But that night the girls turned out to be cock teasers, accepting the drinks and food, all smiles and winks, but refused to go to the hotel with them. When John grew angry, they flagged a cab and left the two Marines frustrated and hard-up on the sidewalk.

There was nothing to do then except return alone to the big, bare hotel room. They removed their heavy drill boots and by habit flicked off the dust before storing them. They hung up their uniforms carefully in the closet, the ties still knotted just right, and threw their sweaty shorts in the corner. At least the shower felt good, but didn't relieve the dull ache in their balls. They went to their respective beds and turned out the light, but a flashing red neon sign outside the window tinged the room intermittently with pink every few seconds.

"John?"

"Yeah?"

"Can you sleep?"

"Naw, my cock keeps digging into the bed. Goddam

1

cock teasers - "

"Yeah, me too."

There were a few moments of silence.

"John?"

"Yeah?"

"Remember that weekend when you went home and I went on liberty alone?"

"Yeah?"

"I told you I made out with a cute chick from La Jolla, but that wasn't quite true."

"Oh?"

"I - uh - had sex with someone from La Jolla, but - it was a guy."

"A guy - a queer?" John's voice revealed his shock at the idea.

"Yeah."

Another few moments of silence.

"So - what happened?" John finally asked, not sure he wanted to hear the story.

"Well," Carl began hesitantly, "I went to all our usual spots that night, and got kinda drunk tryin' to pick up somethin', but no contact - nothin'! I headed back and stopped in the bus station to take a leak. This guy followed me in and watched me takin' a piss, lookin' really interested. I tried to ignore him, but couldn't help gettin' a hard-on. And then he followed me out to the street and asked if he could - uh - take care of me. Well, I was pretty drunk and couldn't get rid of my hard-on, and he was there and anxious for it, and - anyway, I brought him back to the hotel."

Carl lapsed into silence, but John urged him on.

"So what happened?"

"Well - we didn't turn the light on because I didn't really want to see too much, ya' know? But he undressed me, and when he got my pants down he started to fondle my cock with his hands, sort of fluttering movements, and

2

he cupped my balls and stroked it - "

"Fluttering movements?"

"Yeah, sort of - I don't know just how he did it. I tried to do it to myself but I guess it doesn't work that way. Maybe - " Carl broke off. After a moment of silence he continued.

"Maybe - we could do it to each other, what do you think?"

"Well - " John had already tried to "flutter" his cock under the sheets in the darkness, but it didn't seem to do much. "Hell, I suppose it would be OK, just this once. I gotta get some action somewhere!"

Carl left his bed and joined John under his sheet. He reached for his buddy's cock that had formed a small tent. Tentatively he took the stiff pole in one hand and John jerked, the cool hand on his hot meat sending chills up his spine.

Carl only used his thumb and forefinger at first, but when John did not pull away, added more fingers to try to reproduce the "fluttering" movements. John gasped and twisted, the sensations transmitted from his rampant prick throughout his body. His Marine buddy was playing with his dick! The hand was rough but strangely gentle, and his cock lurched with anticipation. But it must be OK - Carl was every inch a man, a Marine!

Hadn't they shared sharp-shooter honors in boot camp? Hadn't they usually tied in their private contests to see which could finish the obstacle course first, and be the first to swim to the far end of the pool after jumping forty feet from the imaginary carrier deck far above? Stand the longest at rigid attention no matter what the weather?

Carl rolled toward John, his stiff prick nudging his buddy's leg.

"Do it to me, buddy," he whispered, the flashing pink lighting up his tortured face.

3

Well, why not? Buddies had to help each other out, didn't they? All the jokes about "your turn in the barrel" were at least half true. It wasn't "queer" that way.

John reached for Carl but his hand became snarled in the sheet. Carl impatiently pulled back the sheet, exposing their muscular, nude bodies to the flickering pink light.

They had seen each other nude countless times, in the shower and even when they were having sex in neighboring beds. But it was somehow different now. Sure, John had always sort of noticed Carl's hard pecs, with the perky little tits sort of asking for attention. And Carl had sort of envied the high ass that pulled John's greens tight into the crease. And their cocks were thick and long as they swung back and forth in the shower sluice, better than most of the guys in the barracks, they thought secretly. But this was different. Their rigid pricks were pointing at each other this time. It was just the two of them together, Marine buddies, fully trusting each other and with no one to watch. They unconsciously waited each time for the momentary illumination from the neon sign to scan the masculine body of their buddy.

John slowly closed his fingers around his buddy's cock, so familiar but yet strange, smooth and pulsing with life and lust. His touch brought an answering jerk, and he began short strokes as Carl was doing for him. Their breathing grew louder as they stiffened and writhed together, the strokes lengthening as they gained confidence. They tried to avoid touching each other except for the rods in their hands, but it was awkward.

"Let's swing around so we don't get in each other's way," Carl suggested, and without waiting for a response, repositioned himself head to foot. Carl began to use both hands, stroking the head of his buddy's cock with one hand as he fluttered and stroked the shaft with the other. John followed suit, still taking direction from his more

4

experienced buddy. They were rigid with growing excitement, their legs moving restlessly and their big pricks responding with jerks and twitches as sensitive spots were caressed. Carl cupped John's balls and fondled them, and John did the same.

"Oh, man, Carl, this is sure better than doin' it alone," John groaned.

"Yeah, it sure is." They whispered hoarsely, their muscles bunching under the masculine touch.

"What else did the guy do?"

"He blew me," Carl answered flatly.

"Yeah? No shit? Was it good?"

"The best I ever had! Hot, wet, all the way down his throat!"

The thought of a hot mouth taking his cock all the way made his dick swell even more, and he tried mentally to substitute that feeling for the rough paw. John stared at Carl's stiff meat in his hand and tried to imagine it in his mouth. But it was so fuckin' big and stiff, how could a guy take it all?

"John?"

"Yeah?" John responded, his breath catching in his throat.

"I did it, too." There, it was finally out.

"You what? You sucked his cock?!"

"Yeah. You won't tell anybody, will you? I don't know - it was there, so close, and my cock felt so fuckin' good in the cocksucker's throat, and I - just wanted to see what it would be like."

It took a few moments for John to accept this. His own Marine buddy, sucking a cock! He realized guiltily that he had just been thinking about doing it, too. And Carl was all man, everybody knew that!

Finally he croaked, "How was it?"

"It was - oh, I don't know, pretty exciting, really. Not dirty or anything. Of course I didn't take it all the way, but the throbbing - and he was suckin' mine at the same time - it was sure better than this hand stuff, I know that!"

"Yeah, I suppose so," John said slowly.

"You want to try it?" Carl asked softly.

"Us? Suck each other?"

"Yeah. I'll do it for you if you do it for me."

"Jeez, I don't know, Carl - "

"Oh, what the hell! Nobody's here to know, and we sure ain't goin' to spread it around. Let's give it a try!"

Still John hesitated, his mind in a whirl.

Getting no definite response, Carl moistened his lips a few inches away from his buddy's throbbing meat. He stared at it, fascinated by the clear pre-cum drooling from the swollen tip. When he stroked toward the head, another dewy drop oozed out and without further thought, his tongue snaked out to taste the sweetness, lapping the head gently.

John lurched, unconsciously attempting to bury it deeper in that tantalizing mouth, and without further thought he took his buddy's cockhead into this mouth. Carl groaned and established that solid connection they both wanted.

They moved closer together, their union joined as they explored their limits that constantly changed. They began to advance further down the shafts, thrilling to the stiff, throbbing maleness in the privacy of the dark room with its flickering light. They gained courage, taking more and more of the pulsing rods with each movement. John felt his cockhead touch the back of Carl's throat and Carl gagged at first, but then stuffed even more of it in! John took Carl as far as he could and felt the throbbing in his throat, the male lust insistent, demanding more!

Carl worked his arm under John's hips and grasped both taut buttocks as he sucked up and down on the rigid rod with increasing fervor. Those prime buns had caught his eye more than once and there they were, in his fevered

6

grasp! John was almost unaware of doing the same until he felt the muscles spasm in his hands. He moved up and down on the smooth cock, going deeper each time, his pleasure soaring. He felt Carl's balls begin to retract, and the cock in his mouth seemed to be growing larger. He pulled up for a moment.

"Guess I ain't very good at this, buddy, but I got to admit, it tastes pretty good," he ventured. "And your hot mouth on me - shit, man - gettin' hotter by the minute!"

Carl really didn't want to stop, but an answer was necessary. "This bone of yours is so fuckin' hot and juicy - maybe there is somethin' to it, ya know?" And then, as John tried to cram it all in his throat, he returned to his task - but only for a moment. He groaned loudly, stiffened tensely, and pulled up again.

"Take it, Marine! I'm goin' to cum in your mouth! Take my juice!" He thrust hard and deep into his buddy's throat, and dove down once again on the rigid rammer begging for his mouth.

John did not hesitate a moment. The stiff prick was going to shoot in his mouth and he was ordered to take it! There was no opportunity for thought.

The first spurt struck with force, and he choked and sputtered, but at that moment he released his torrent into Carl's throat as they gripped each other tightly. Hot, sweet, spicy cream - man juice spurting, giving to each other, sharing their bodies man to man! Suddenly it was important not to fail, important that they take what their buddy offered and make it good, as good as it was for each of them. At this point the most important thing in the world was their flooding cocks in their furiously sucking mouths.

They gulped the heady nectar down as if starved, as if they had saved it up for just this occasion, all that virility worthy only of a buddy, another Marine. They saluted each other with their prime essence of manhood, and felt equally matched as usual in all things important in a man. Only after the torrents had ceased and the cocks began to sag was the connection broken.

They looked up at each other and smiled, eager to believe that things were as they had always been, but knowing they would never be the same again. John stroked Carl's drooping cock, bringing another drop of pearly essence to the tip. He licked it off, savoring the taste of his buddy before he rested his head on the muscular leg.

After a moment, John spoke again. "Hey - you know what else we did...?"

THE END

MONTANA TRYST

Chad finished his second cup of coffee boiled over the campfire and washed up the frying pan used for his bacon breakfast. He lashed the cooking utensils and his bedroll to his horse and continued the repair work on the ranch fence. As far as the eye could see, the barbed wire stretched across acres of rolling Montana hills freshly green in the budding spring. Since he was working alone and it was a routine task, pounding fence posts and tightening the wire, he had plenty of time to think about the experiences of the last few days and his introduction to sex, cowboy style.

Sexually he had been dormant, it seemed, all his life as if waiting for something to happen. His experiences with women had been few, but those he had were rather dull. His reaction was sort of, ho-hum, is that all there is? That is, until recently when his senses were awakened by his fellow ranchhands in ways that still boggled his mind. And his own spontaneous reactions were also shocking - he would never forget his initiation into the "Montana" scene.

Last week he had started his first job away from home as the new hand at the Twin Circles Ranch. He was assigned to the far end of the bunkhouse housing six other men, all older and more experienced and apparently friends for several years. It was his first experience living closely with other men, and he had blushed furiously when one of them made a playful grab at his long, thick cock when he had undressed his first night there. He received some inquisitive looks at this negative reaction, and after that they seemed to leave him alone. The young blond with the broad shoulders, slim waist, and huge bulge down the leg of his levis would have been a tasty morsel, but they weren't going to push the point too far.

9

Although confused by his own responses, he wasn't so sure he wanted to be left alone...

The first morning after his arrival he rose early, thinking he would be the first one in the shower so he could lose his morning hard-on before the others were up. But when he approached the communal shower room, he heard the water running. He peeked cautiously around the corner of the door, and what he saw made his boner even harder. Rocky, the dark, bearded foreman, and Cord, his closest friend, were already there. Rocky stood under the pounding spray, his hairy fists on his hips and eyes closed, while Cord knelt at his feet sucking his huge cock as if it was breakfast!

Chad watched the warm lips engulf the broad head and travel down the shaft, the cowboy's thick tongue caressing the prominent veins and muscular stalk with practiced skill. Rocky groaned with the exquisite pleasure and placed a hand gently on the bobbing head. Temporarily leaving the thick rod, Cord gripped the pendulous balls, squeezing them into a tight sphere of fur-covered morsels, and began to lap and lick them, rolling them from side to side.

"Yeah, suck 'em, man, be good to those balls. They're goin' to give you a load soon - " Rocky moaned, the water streaming down his hairy chest and thickly-muscled legs taut from the tantalizing touch. He began to stroke himself slowly.

"You just let me handle that buckin' bronco," Cord cautioned and returned to his work.

Chad gasped. These guys were the most masculine bunch he had ever encountered, and it never occurred to him that they might be - like that. Suddenly his mind flashed back to a recurring dream, where cowboys without faces stood over him, jerking off in great gobs over him, the cum pooling on his chest and belly, running in rivulets down his sides. He always woke up, cock twitching and

10

wet, embarrassed at his secret fantasies.

"Take that prick, Cord, go ahead, suck it down!" Rocky commanded. "I want to feel it all the way down your cocksuckin' throat!"

Quickly Cord abandoned his ball worship and shifted back to the huge cock throbbing above. He shoved that tool all the way down, the broad head spreading his throat until he almost choked, and then set up an up-and-down motion that curled his boss's toes. Cord's fist was working on his own prick that extended almost to the streaming floor of the shower.

Chad grabbed his own cock that was violently stabbing the air. His bulging cockhead was moist with pre-cum. His clammy hand didn't feel like that hot mouth must feel, but it was all he had. Rocky's eyes were still closed, and so far Chad was apparently unobserved.

"Oh, Christ, yeah - take it!" Rocky groaned loudly, Cord's mouth bringing him to that pounding point. "Suck it, man, take that fuckin' cum!" His body quivered with lust and need.

Cord gurgled happily as he took the hot spurts, and his own cock exploded in streams of joy between his legs. Rocky thrust forward, filling his mouth to overflowing with manjuice as Cord's cream curdled and swirled in the flooding water.

Chad was only seconds behind them. He quickly darted to the urinal and shot streams of gism into the white trough, shaking violently from his first exposure to man-to-man sex. He clung to the plumbing for support, his knees buckling. When he finally stopped shaking and drained the last drops from his softening prick, he flushed the urinal noisily before entering the shower. The two men were grinning at each other, arms on the other's shoulder, and did not seem at all embarrassed at his entry.

And then it was only a couple of days later that he was again startled by sex Montana style. The men had worked together on the range that day, repairing fences and clearing streams clogged with brush deposited by the spring rains. They had eaten a hearty supper from the chuck wagon and taken to their bedrolls under a starry sky. Chad had wandered away from the dying campfire, thinking he would be more private in a clump of cottonwoods near by, but apparently Jack and Bart had had the same idea.

"Come on, Jack, nobody's goin' to interrupt us here. I been droolin' over your hot ass all day, and you know you want it! Come here and sit on it!"

Chad quickly drew back into the shadows, easing his bedroll to the ground silently. At first he was disappointed that he would not be alone, but the overheard conversation sparked his interest.

"I don't know whether I can take you or not, Bart, you horny bastard - I ain't much used to gettin' plugged, ya know - " Jack answered uncertainly.

Bart gripped his pole with a hairy fist and shook it at his buddy, the moist head glistening in the faint light as Chad watched, his own cock lengthening in his levis. He noticed that Bart was shedding his clothes as he stared at the offered meat, not so reluctant as he seemed. His white, round ass contrasted sharply with his chest and back, darkened from working in the sun all day. His own cock bounced free and clear.

"It ain't so big, see?" Bart waved his long dong tantalizingly at his buddy. "And I really hanker that hot hole. Come here, man, let me eat it and get you ready."

No longer hesitant, Jack moved to straddle his buddy and lowered himself toward his buddy's face. Bart groaned as he feasted his eyes on that beckoning crack and then, pulling Jack close, began to feast in earnest, his tongue probing deep into the hairy ass hole.

Again Chad was shocked, his own ass hole beginning to twitch with the sight. Jack's cock and balls rested on

12

his friend's face, and his head was thrown back in obvious ecstasy from the intimate invasion. Chad quickly lowered his own levis, his cock gripped in a tense fist, totally oblivious to the night cricket sounds and warm breeze rustling through the trees.

"Yeah, man, eat it," Jack gritted as his buddy pulled him tight against his face. Bart's slurps were incoherent testimony of his pleasure, and he stroked his own cock slowly as Chad watched. Tentatively Chad reached around and circled his own puckered ass hole with a finger tip, wondering what it would be like to be served in that way. It felt good, but dry.

Then Jack raised up and moved back. "I'm goin' to cum if you keep that up. Stick that big poker in me, Bart, you fucker! Gimme your fuckin' meat!" He spat in his hand and spread it over the head of his buddy's cock and then gradually lowered himself until the flaring head was at his opening. He adjusted his position slightly and then sank down slowly, the thick prick disappearing into his nether regions.

"Oh, Christ, that's good," Bart gasped. "So fuckin' hot, so tight, oh yeah..."

Jack's face revealed the strain he was under. He grimaced and frowned but did not stop. He wanted that dick up his chute as much as Bart wanted it there. Not until he felt the scratchy pubic hair pressing and the hairy balls mashing against him did he stop his downward progression.

Chad advanced his finger deeper into his own ass, trying to capture the feeling. Surprisingly it didn't really hurt, but it was tight around his finger. What must that thick prick feel like?

Bart began to thrust upward into his hot buddy, driving his prick deep into the secret channel. Jack began to bounce with each thrust, the cock shoving in and out faster and faster as they struggled together. Bart gripped

13

the sparse grass in fistfuls, but his eyes never left Jack's, holding him in a rivetting gaze of love and lust.

Jack began to jerk his own cock rapidly as did Chad still hidden in the shadows. Chad twisted his finger in his own ass hole, feeling twinges of heat and joy course through his straining body.

"Oh, shit, I'm goin' to shoot - goin' to fill your ass, buddy," Bart grunted, never slowing his heavy thrusting.

"Yeah, do it, Bart - goin' to shoot all over your belly, you big fucker," Jack responded. "Yeah! Here it comes! Fuckin' hot cum all over ya!"

"Give it to me, man," Bart growled, his legs trembling and jerking as his climax began.

"Ah! Ah! Oh, yeah!" their scrambled voices jumbled through clenching teeth. "Yeah!" Chad groaned more softly, his own cum splattering a young tree as Jack's spurted in gobs onto Bart's hairy chest. Three cocks jerking wildly in delirious pleasure, cum splashing and squirting in the spring night!

As the coupled cowboys calmed at last, they sagged together. Chad had only the tree for support. Bart scooped up some cum from his chest and brought it to his mouth, relishing it from his fingers. They grinned happily at each other. Still shaking, Chad pulled his levis up and returned to the others nearer the fire.

The next day the men separated, taking individual fence runs alone and planning to meet again at the ranch when they were finished. As the sun rose in the sky, Chad worked his way up the mountain, and could catch glimpses of the Twin Circles Ranch in the distance. He had been told that the ranch section of the fence ended near a spring and marked by a pole gate; from there on the fence belonged to an Indian rancher who owned the property on the other side.

In the heat of the day, his clothes began to stick to his body. He removed his shirt, and then finally also his

14

levis, wearing only his hat and boots as he worked. His long cock slapped against his thighs as he worked, constantly semi-hard from reliving those voyeuristic moments. He gnawed on hard tack for lunch and drank from the canteen filled from the stream the night before.

As he worked his way over a small rise he saw ahead the gate that must be the end of his section of fence. He also heard dimly the burble of a stream on the other side of the fence, and suddenly he realized he was thirsty. He unhooked the canteen from the saddle and squeezed through the fence, careful not to snag his bare skin on the barbs, heading for the sound of the stream.

As he came out of a clump of cottonwood trees into a clearing, he stopped short. Water gushed from the ground forming a fairly deep pool almost hidden by the low-hanging branches of a huge old willow tree. In the pool, staring straight at him, stood a young Indian, totally nude. He had apparently heard Chad approach so was not surprised by his appearance.

The young man stood looking Chad up and down. He was lithe, copper-skinned and muscular with straight black hair extending down to the nape of his neck. His eyes were also black, wide spaced, over a strong, straight nose. His lips were rather thick, and as Chad watched they parted in a small smile revealing pure white teeth. His shoulders were strong and broad, and every muscle in his arms, chest, and belly was clearly defined as if carved from bronze. His hips were unbelievably slim, but the legs swelled to bronze columns of strapping muscle. His nipples were like dark medals on a hairless chest, but below his navel a veritable bush of wiry black hair framed a long, pendulous cock. Standing there in the pool, surrounded by budding trees and spring foliage, he seemed a part of nature, a beautiful creature belonging to the mountains and streams.

Chad's eyes returned to the crotch. As he gazed it

15

gave a twitch and the cockhead began to emerge from the foreskin, the muscle growing and rising majestically.

Chad's eyes rose to meet the Indian's. The smile had broadened but the black eyes were now fixed on Chad's cock. Suddenly Chad realized that his own cock was growing, too, as he stood mute in the dappled shadow of the willow. He watched as the Indian's cockhead emerged from the foreskin and became completely revealed, the dark pink mushroom pointing directly at him. The cock was about the same size as Chad's, thick and strong. Neither had spoken a word.

The Indian raised one hand slowly. It resembled an invitation from an emperor to join him in his bath.

Chad hesitated only a minute, and then dropped the canteen, shed his boots and hat, and slowly advanced into the pool. The Indian's hand was still extended; their gazes were locked together. Chad drew near until their stiff cocks almost touched above the cool water. He grasped the proffered hand firmly, not in a handshake but in some tactile greeting that both understood. There was communication in the touch - spiritual contact between virile embodiments of nature. It seemed as if both had been waiting a long time for that moment.

The Indian suddenly pulled Chad toward him as he splashed down in the water. Chad came up choking and laughing, and then it was his turn to upset the Indian. They splashed and rolled in the spring pool, grasping for arms and legs and buttocks, their cocks touching momentarily. And then they stood suddenly quiet, holding each other's cock, their eyes searching the other's face for signs of withdrawal, disapproval, disgust - Both saw only agreement and excitement and involvement.

Again the Indian led the way. Still holding the blond cowboy by the cock, he led the way to a tiny sand and grass beach at the edge of the pool. They squatted cross-legged facing each other, each fondling the other's

16

matching prick. There was no awkwardness, no urgency, only the joy of discovery, of immediate intimacy, of brotherhood. At last the Indian broke the spell of silence.

"I will kiss your beautiful cock." It was a flat statement spoken in a soft, low musical voice. He watched Chad's eyes as he spoke.

"Yes," Chad answered simply, soberly.

Slowly the Indian leaned toward Chad and lowered his head between their legs which were now touching. The long, pink cock bobbed its head up to meet the dark lips. The full mouth descended slowly on the cock, savoring the contact, the tongue moving tentatively and wonderingly as it went.

"Ahhh," Chad sighed as the warmth covered him.

He still held the rigid staff of the Indian, but the Indian's hand now pressed gently against his chest, requesting his surrender to the oral lovemaking. Almost reluctantly Chad lay back, sinking into the warmth of the boy of the mountain.

The Indian moved forward on his knees and took the cock all the way to the base, resting his chin on Chad's large balls. Chad gasped and began to tremble slightly as he watched in fascination. He felt engulfed in a moist, welcoming warmth that touched the core of his being. He was afraid to move, wanting more and more but aware of the importance of the moment, a moment that must not be disturbed. The dark head lifted and dropped again, tonguing and sucking languorously as the lips applied gentle pressure. There was total involvement and devotion in his movements. Then he raised his head and their eyes met and held again, the Indian settling back on his haunches.

Chad pulled his gaze away from the magnetic orbs. He reached for the thick cock towering from the dark bush. He watched the pink cockhead appear and almost disappear as the slowly stroked the foreskin hypnotically.

17

Although it was the first time to grasp another man's cock, it felt right and natural. There was a question in the Indian's eyes.

In answer, Chad said softly, "This is the first time for me."

The Indian breathed, "Yes." That was all.

Chad bent to hold the thick cock close to his face, caressing it, watching the clear viscous fluid form on the tip and become silver strands to the sand. His tongue moistened his lips but he hesitated. What would it taste like? Would he choke? Would he be able to please this strange, fascinating creature? The Indian waited patiently, his eyes following the flickers of thought crossing Chad's face.

Then the cowboy simply lowered his head and took the bronze cock in his mouth. There was no thought of right or wrong, or sin, or shame, or guilt. It was right to do this at this time in this place with this special person. It was not even a sexual gesture in the sense of promoting orgasm. It was sensual, and masculine, and loving.

Chad thrilled to the smooth, warm, stiff member in his mouth. As the skin moved back, the hotter cockhead met his tongue; he licked all around it, fascinated by the sometimes hidden beacon. Then he pulled the foreskin back to cover the head, tasting again, before inching his way down the warm shaft.

The Indian tensed but watched silently, intently, supporting himself on one elbow. Occasional small jerks of his body were the only indication of reaction, but he was careful not to disturb the contact. A hum started in the Indian's throat and increased in volume as the hot mouth descended. Chad was becoming more and more excited by the young man's response but could not interpret all the silent messages. He loved the sensuous texture of the smooth cock and the warm throbbing in his mouth. He continued down until the head touched the back of his throat. There was no discomfort, only a question of how to proceed, how to take the remaining flesh. He must have it all! It was vital that this be good for the boy, but he knew not why.

The Indian placed a gentle hand on his head, a signal to go easily. Chad slid up the shaft and took a breath. The Indian nodded. Again he gently pushed Chad back and took him to the hilt, moving his legs toward Chad's head and stretching out in the sand. He began to suck the beautiful stiff prick, grasping Chad's golden buttocks in both copper hands. He possessed him totally.

Chad imitated the Indian's actions and resumed his exploration of the copper cock now closer to him. He gripped the firm buttocks and pulled them to him, taking most of the cock as deeply as he could. This total connection, total involvement in giving and taking, sent his brain spinning! Never had he experienced such intimacy. The sensations in his cock were rapturous, but the combination with the Indian's cock in his mouth at the same time, completing the circuit, blocked all other thoughts from his mind. Nothing existed except the two young men, giving and receiving, together!

They pulled closer together, their bellies touching, roughened hands exploring and caressing their backs, the muscles tensing under copper and suntanned skin. Their fingertips dipped into the cleft between tense ass cheeks and over the mounds of the muscles. The contrast between the coloration, the blond, almost silvery cowboy and the bronzed sinewy Indian were worthy of an artist's easel. Chad learned that he could take the entire cock into his throat without difficulty because he wanted to, wanted it very much.

The Indian slid off the cockhead and down the shaft, his tongue flicking, to the ball sack with its fine, blond fur. He moistened the sack with his tongue and gently sucked one globe into his mouth, rolling it from side to side. Then he released it to treat the other one to the same gentle ministrations. Chad moaned with the new sensation and followed suit. The Indian's balls were unusually large, and one was a mouthful. He stroked the long, moist shaft as he sucked first one and then the other.

A sudden urgency came upon them. The time was past for exploring. Their lust for each other was beginning to soar and was not to be denied! Both turned their attentions to the stiff, throbbing pricks, beginning to suck ferociously, the cocks swelling even more with the heightened tension.

The continuous circuit was under pressure now. The copper arm pressed the pink-white body against his dark, muscular frame. Chad hugged the copper mounds roughly, pulling the darker body to his face, compelled to take all it could give. Both heads moved in unison, faster and faster. Chad's teeth scraped a little but it didn't matter, it was too important to allow details to distract from the enormity of their desire. There was only one possible conclusion, and it was demanded, it was inescapable, now!

Chad's orgasm started only a split second before the Indian's, and he gasped just as the first spurt occurred. He choked with the hot, sweet cum suddenly flooding his throat, but recovered quickly. He was enthralled by the sweet-salty taste of the Indian's cream, but at that moment he would have accepted it gladly even if it had tasted terrible. This was too important! His entire body was wracked with the violence of his own orgasm, accentuated by the thrill of the continuing spurts of love juice from the dark cock already so precious to him.

A bond was established in the few minutes of that mutual orgasm that would never be broken. Even as the cocks softened in the still mouths, the connection remained. The cocks shrank but were not released. It was ended but still continuing somehow. When they finally disconnected, they knew it was only a temporary interruption until the next stage could begin.

The Indian swung around and took Chad in his arms. Each saw love and joy and discovery in the other's face. They kissed deeply, gratefully, joyfully, their soft wet cocks mashed together, never thinking that the action was strange or new. It was right and deeply satisfying. A decision had been made but they were only vaguely aware of their sense of commitment at that time.

"I'm Chad."

"I'm Buck."

It did not occur to them that it was strange to introduce themselves after their tempestuous lovemaking. It was merely a detail to facilitate communication.

"I feel that I love you," Buck said slowly.

"I feel the same," Chad responded.

"Can men love each other, do you think?" asked Buck.

"We do, therefore they can," Chad smiled.

"Yes," Buck said simply, drawing Chad's face to him for another long kiss of commitment. In their simplicity, everything was settled.

They began to talk about their lives before that special moment, discovering that they were approximately the same age, and that Buck lived on the ranch next to the Twin Circles which was actually visible about an hour's ride from their trysting place. Chad's observations of the other cowboys never entered his head. Somehow that was another world. Buck was a light shining in space limited by the low-hanging branches of the willow tree beside the pool.

Chad rummaged in his pack and brought out a shiny disk of steel on a leather thong which he always carried with him as a good luck charm. He presented it to Buck.

"I want you to have this," he said. "Perhaps it has

brought me you." The young man accepted it silently, his eyes full of love, and momentarily brought it to his lips.

Buck suddenly leaped to his feet and started doing handsprings in circles around Chad who laughed merrily. Buck splashed into the pool, rolling around the pebbly bottom, then jumped up again, his face split in a wide grin.

"You! You're beautiful! And you love me!" The dripping water turned his copper skin to gold in the light of the red, setting sun.

"How did I find you? How did you find me?" His wonderment was mixed with joy; his exuberance was contagious. He dropped to one knee and caressed the face and strong chin of his lover in wonder and awe.

"You appeared from the trees with a golden glow - your hair, your skin the color of the sun. Are you really here now or is it an illusion? Are you real, Chad lover?"

Chad answered, "You appeared from a mountain pool, your body a part of nature. Your beautiful cock uncapped its head and pointed to me. My body answered with no hesitation. We are real, Buck lover."

Long moments passed as they explored each other's body, their gaze never breaking. Then they suddenly realized that they were becoming chilled as the sun set and the evening breeze brushed their moist skins. They made camp in the clearing and built a roaring fire. Still nude, each watched the muscle play of the other's body as they performed their tasks. They staked out the horses to graze and shared their remaining food. Every movement, every gesture, was addressed to the other. Chad thought he had never seen such a beautiful human being; he was dark where Chad was light, especially in the light of the fire, and he moved with a natural grace that reminded Chad of the deer seen occasionally in these mountains.

They combined their bedrolls and lay closely together

near the fire. Their cocks were constantly erect, but sex was not vital now. They were learning about each other with subtle, unspoken communication. They both kept returning to a summary word.

"Love."

There was no thought of practicality. They were together, it was right, it was inescapable! It was awesome.

The stiff cocks bumped heads. Buck took both of them in his hand and caressed them together, causing both lean bodies to tense in anticipation.

"Do you want me again?"

"I want you very much."

"Buck?"

"Yes?"

"Will you fuck me?"

"Is it - all right?"

"I - don't know. I think so. Yes! I want you!"

Buck pulled the blond face to him and kissed him with promise. Then he began to lick the bulging muscles of his lover's chest and nibbled on the tiny nipples, twirling his tongue in the shallow navel. Chad twisted and squirmed. And then the moist tongue played in the light pubic hair and caressed the groin crease.

He suddenly shifted tactics, swooping down on the rigid pink pole, causing Chad to groan and arch his back for more. But Buck stopped to lap the heavy balls below, then shifting to the bulging thighs, teasing the silky golden hair and following the outline of the tense cords.

Buck moved between Chad's legs and lifted them to his shoulders, beginning again on the heavy balls. Then rocking his lover's hips back, his tongue traced lower, causing a quiver in Chad's frame. Still quivering, the cowboy felt his legs spread wide and straight, bringing the tiny pink opening to view.

Buck smiled into his lover's eyes. "It's beautiful," he

said softly.

"It's yours," Chad responded, and closed his eyes.

Buck began to nibble on the firm ass cheeks, moving in narrowing circles and eventually zeroing in on the puckered muscle. When his tongue touched the opening, Chad moaned and squirmed. Buck increased the vigor of his approach, kissing and licking and probing the tiny rosette until it began to relax. As he could, he advanced further and further into his lover, circling the opening with a stiffened tongue. Chad moaned and begged for more, writhing in joy and frustration. He needed Buck inside him!

"Please!" he begged, his head tossing, his eyes closed in fantasy.

"Yes," the Indian promised, placing a last kiss on this most valued possession, leaving excess saliva behind.

He hunkered closer and placed his cockhead against the opening but then hesitated. Chad's eyes opened, his gaze burning into the dark eyes above.

"Fuck," he said calmly.

Buck shoved in past the sphincter in one movement. Chad jerked and grimaced, then relaxed again.

"Fuck," Chad said again, composed but demanding. His eyes closed again.

Buck shoved his huge prick in all the way with a slow, steady, constant pressure. This was another world from his exploring finger while he watched the cowboys in the cottonwood grove. This was Buck! Chad refused to resist, willing his lover's entry as a promise to fulfill, and when he was completely filled, a smile began to flood his face, a smile that left no doubt as to his feelings.

Buck began to rotate his hips with the cock fully embedded. His lover's smile grew. Buck felt the inner core of his lover caressing his stiff cock, and the smile on the cowboy's face told him of the pleasure he was bringing him. The black pubic hair mixed with the blond strands on his lover's ball sack.

Chad's eyes opened. He was totally at peace with his dark lover engulfed in his body. Now he wanted to see as well as feel. The Indian's dark eyes expressed his returned love. The smile on his usually sober face revealed the pleasure Chad was providing him. The muscles of his chest and arms glistened in the flickering firelight.

"Love," whispered Chad.

"Love," answered his lover.

"Fuck."

"Now."

Buck pulled almost all the way out and, without seeming to stop the movement, shoved in all the way again. His movements were swinging and rhythmic, almost like dancing. Chad's ass seemed to flutter and kiss the Indian's cock as it moved in and out with liquid grace. It was hot and tender and virile! The blond lover almost sang with joy to possess and be possessed in this most intimate of all possible lovemaking.

Unconsciously he began to move with the rhythm, his ass meeting his lover with each movement. Buck's smile broadened and his eyes took on a glassy look. He picked up speed, the teasing over.

"Hard," smiled Chad.

"Yes," Buck agreed as he began to ram harder and harder.

"Harder!" gritted Chad.

"Ugh," Buck groaned. "Ugh - Ugh - Ugh -" with each thrust.

"Love," Chad groaned loudly.

"Love!" Buck shouted. His muscles were bulging, his trim buttocks in rigid spasms as he plunged in and out.

"Cock! - Ass!"

"Ass - Fuck - Love!"

"Love!"

Their grunted words were overlapping, both men only half aware that they were making any sounds. The words were punctuations of their actions which were bringing them close to the brink. Buck's prick rode in and out like a locomotive.

When they both felt their culminations approach, Buck's cock swelled even more and Chad's movements became jerky. He had not even touched his cock, but it was jerking and throbbing against his belly.

"Fuck! - Cum!"

"Cum! - Love!"

"Cuming!"

"Shoot! - Cum!"

"Cum! - Ahhhhhhh - CUM!"

Buck came in a gush into his lover's hot clenching ass. The plunging prick plundered the pulsating pathway, filling his lover with its body and spirit. Chad moaned with joy at each jerk of the cock inside him. This was the ultimate in love, ecstasy, fulfillment! And suddenly the cowboy's waving prick began to jet its juice over Chad's belly, bringing him to the peak of rapture with the simultaneous sensations flooding over him.

Buck bent his lithe body and swooped down to take the shooting prick deep into his mouth. He could not miss the precious cream of his lover! It was meant for him! He continued to move in and out as he sucked and swallowed the nectar. Even after there was no more he held the spent cock in his throat, his eyes closed in gratitude to the gods.

They slept closely clasped in each other's arms, the outside world shut out.

They had sex again in the morning, a slow, deliberate, masculine exchange of love and passion and promise, knowing both would have to return to their homes. Buck took out the shiny disk that Chad had given him.

"Whenever I can, I will return here. You will know

I am here when you see the sun glinting from your precious disc, hanging from the top of our willow tree. I will wait for you to come to me."

"I will come to you," Chad responded, his spirit soaring. And the bond was sealed.

THE END

Bonds struck
under weeping willow trees
are as solid as oaks and
everlasting as the redwood.

MECHANICS MADNESS

Ron's eyes feasted on the succulent, rounded ass. Leaning into the engine compartment of the huge 1959 Caddy, as Jim was then doing, stretched his already tight, faded levis to their utmost, and set Ron's cock twitching with familiar desire for the hunky young mechanic in the auto repair garage where they both worked. And even more enticing, the top of the crack of that beautiful ass was showing above the levi waistband!

It was very quiet in the garage, since the rest of the men had left for the day. Jim had promised a good customer to finish the job of tuning up the old Caddy, although it meant working overtime, and Ron had decided to stay late on a private job of his own. Also it helped to have another guy around in case of problems needing two people to handle. But working close to Jim in the deserted garage could be pretty unsettling, Ron was beginning to discover.

Jim leaned even further down, one foot off the floor, to reach a difficult spot. The levis inched down even further, and Ron could see a few brown hairs in that crevice leading to nirvana. He forgot about his project, his mind concentrating on the lure of that golden crease only a couple of feet away.

Jim was concentrating on his work, with a few stifled grunts at some stubborn fitting. He would never notice a little touch, Ron reasoned. Tentatively he ran his fingertips over the bare back of his buddy between levis and loose T-shirt. The skin was smooth and warm, seeming warmer below the distinct tan line than above where it was golden brown. There was no reaction from Jim, although he must be aware of the touch.

Ron's fingertip dipped into the crease and back out hurriedly. Still no response. He grew a little bolder, running his fingers down the valley to the stretched top of the levis. There was a quiet grunt from Jim, not unlike those occasionally heard before as he struggled with the old car. That was all.

Ron's cock started to swell, so close and yet so far from his most desired goal. After a few more strokes and still meeting no resistance, he inserted his finger under the waistband as far as it would go, feeling the heat of the sweaty ass radiating upward. Still no resistance.

He bent close to that enticing entrance, picking up the musky aroma of mansweat, grease, and crotch all mixed together. That combination should be bottled, he decided, if the effect it had on his own libido was any indication. He took deep breaths and reveled in the excitement they generated. Cautiously he pulled the waistband out a little to insert his nose deeper, getting even a stronger whiff of Jim's most private possessions. The mechanic did not move, but continued his ministrations to the aging engine.

He's got to know I'm playing around, Ron reasoned. Since he doesn't object, he must have decided to go along! Nobody knows about me in this garage. If I take a chance, go for broke, the word might get around and I'll be out on my ass. On the other hand...

His hands were shaking, but Ron found the situation irresistible. He couldn't give up now when he was so fuckin' close!

Gently, as unobtrusively as possible, he reached around to Jim's front and slowly unbuttoned the top of the fly. Jim wasn't wearing any belt, so that was no problem. As soon as the button was released, there was another inch free at the back and the levis slipped down even further. Quickly Ron breathed in the aroma, his prick rigid in his own levis. So fuckin' hot, so masculine, so tantalizing! Maybe one more button wouldn't hurt...?

Another button slipped its moorings, but there was

less territory gained that time. Maybe another button... and another inch opened up, another precious strip of bare ass was revealed to Ron's quickening response. He could almost see the ultimate quest, that dark rosette he needed so much.

Now that the goal was almost in sight, he couldn't stop now. Another button, slowly freeing it, gently teasing the levis open, and there it was! The levis were free and slipped easily down over the round buns, white in sharp contrast to the dark tan above, bulging with tense muscles from the bent posture, split down the middle with the most enticing ass crease Ron had ever seen. A few brown hairs were sprinkled in that crease, and a few more encircled the darker aperture that demanded attention! And still no objection from his buddy.

Ron struggled his own rigid rod out of his levis and began to stroke it slowly as he surveyed the beauty before him. He knelt inches away from that promised land, placing his nose within millimeters of that tight asshole and breathing in the funky aroma. An aphrodisiac if there ever was one!

Jim moved back slightly, enough to get both feet on the floor, and almost cracked Ron's nose in the process. The change in position brought the ass muscles in even sharper relief, and the levis slipped down even further. Was he making it easier for Ron to do - whatever he was going to do?

Ron couldn't hold back now. His tongue snaked out and lapped that beckoning beacon, picking up the rich taste of sweaty asshole that set his tastebuds dancing. Another lap added to the first. There was another soft grunt from Jim - did that mean approval? Ron's cock jerked in his grease-smudged fist. Another couple of swipes with his tongue left glistening saliva to mark the spot.

Gently Ron pulled down on the legs of the levis,

exposing most of the hairy, tanned thighs. The lower tan line was just below the fold of the buttocks, and Ron's tongue did not leave these landmarks ignored. He lapped along both thighs and up over the curves, back into the crease, and probed deeper into the asshole that was going to be his! He thrilled to the sweetness, the virgin freshness of his buddy's inner core, probing deeply and avidly. The ass opened slowly, invitingly, urging him silently to gorge himself on the secret storehouse. Soon his entire tongue was inside, the slick slot swimming with juice.

Then he moved down, tasting the forbidden fruit that were still untouched. He encountered two packed balls, hairy and swollen, and gave them a couple of laps also. One hand inserted beyond them, and he had a growing stalk of thick prick in his grasp which he pulled down lovingly. Big, fuckin' prick! A bulbous head partly covered with foreskin, already oozing a little encouraging pre-cum as he stroked it slowly but firmly. When he returned to the asshole, dipping deeper and more aggressively, he felt the cock jerk in his grip. Christ, what a man! And he was his for the taking!

The silence was only broken by Ron's heavy breathing. Forgotten were the facts that the garage door was open, and it wouldn't have taken much effort for someone to walk in and look around the cars and see the action between them. That the boss might stop by to see how they were coming (cuming!) at any minute. That the silly cashier girl might check in with them before leaving for the night.

Slowly Ron rose to his feet, his cock protruding straight and true. He had gotten this far, but would he make it all the way? He had to try!

He collected some saliva in his hand and spread it over his own cock. Soon his own nine inches of meat were slick and shiny, with extra on the head. Gently he pressed it against the tiny opening that seemed more relaxed than before. There was no reaction so he pressed harder. He watched his cockhead slowly advance into the opening asshole, and the ass cheeks begin to tremble slightly.

As the head disappeared, it was consumed in heat, grasping, gripping, welcoming warmth, and as he continued to press onward, his entire prick was swallowed up in Jim's moist manhole. "Oh, shit, so fuckin' good," Ron moaned, shoving the last couple of inches in to feel his balls press against the manly rear. His own blond pubic hairs mixed with the golden ones, grating the tender skin luxuriously.

He let it soak there for a minute, afraid that he would cum immediately and cut short the fantastic experience. His knees trembled with the enormity of his actions, his rigid ramrod buried in his buddy's ass.

Still immersed to the hilt, he ran his hands up under Jim's T-shirt, over the taut, ridged belly muscles, to the bulging pecks covered with crisp, curly hair. He gripped the tiny rosebuds of tits perched there, feeling them tense and protrude under his touch. He pinched them gently, and felt an answering backward thrust of the ass, indicating pleasure and perhaps impatience - to get on with it!

Then it was unavoidable. He had to move, had to thrust in and out, had to fuck that hot ass denied him for so long. He pulled halfway out and moved in again, and the resulting clamor in his brain called for more and more of the same! He picked up his rhythm, thrusting in and out, his buddy answering him with low moans and gentle claspings of his ass channel. Ron pulled harder on his tits as he began to slam in and out, making the old Caddy groan as its creaky suspension was brought into action.

Ron shifted from the tits to the balls and cock hanging low between his buddy's legs. He gripped the balls in one hand and the cock in the other, all of his buddy's goodies

33

under his control. Again that pleasured groan, louder this time, signifying his surrender of all he had to offer.

Too soon, Ron felt the rumblings of climax building. He stopped, but that ass was so hot, so tight, so fuckin' sweet, that he might still go over the top. Reluctantly he pulled out, his cock jerking and threatening to explode until he took a few shaky breaths.

He quickly knelt down and pulled back on the thick stalk in his hand. He began to lap the engorged mushroom, the pre-cum sweet on his tongue. He pulled the foreskin down and ran his tongue under the fold, all around the head, and Jim again groaned with approval. Then pushing the foreskin back to expose the entire cockhead, he began to suck furiously, feeling the cock swell and jerk in his mouth.

From behind he could only get about five inches of dick in his mouth, but there were probably another five inches above that. Hard, throbbing dick, needing a man's mouth, needing a draining of its crankcase.

"Beautiful prick," he murmured, thrilling to the manly taste and odor of working man's crotch. His nose nudged the heavy balls on either side and he lapped them a few times for good measure, wetting the golden hairs covering them, before returning to the stiff fuckstick. His own cock was in his fist, but he dare not stroke it for danger of explosion.

His other hand sought the asshole above, and he inserted one finger into the heat of that ravenous furnace. So tight but so accepting! He pushed in until he felt the rounded bulge of the prostrate, and as he traced its outline, Jim moaned louder, pushing against him with pent-up desire. Ron's mouth on his dick and his finger in his asshole was too much to remain silent! And Ron couldn't stand the tension much longer, either.

Substituting his hand for his mouth on Jim's cock, Ron rose and again entered the beckoning asshole. This time

34

he pressed in in one movement, the ass swallowing him avidly. This time there was no holding back - he shifted to overdrive and began to fuck in rapid, pistoning thrusts, ravishing that beautiful asshole with his supercharger while he jerked the stiff prick below.

Jim's groans increased, needing, begging for his buddy's load, his cock jerking and thrusting in its drive for the ultimate. And it was not long in coming. Ron felt his balls pull up and knew there was no turning back, it was now, now - blast off!

"Ahhhhhh!" he yelled, his first spurt shaking him from head to toe, the heated ass sucking his cum from his tortured balls like a siphon sucks gas from a tank. He slammed into his buddy, and his second spurt flooded his hot, steaming ass. And at that moment, Jim let loose with a jet from his own prick still gripped in Ron's greasy fist.

The Caddy rocked with the action, the mechanic shoved against it, his ass full of squirting prick, his cock giving its all to the demanding fist. The men's groans blended with the complaining squeaks of the Caddy springs as they struggled on that rocky road to bliss.

"Yeah! Fuckin' your hot ass, Jim, givin' it to ya," Ron gritted, his knees rigid as steel, his buddy's cum flooding his hand and pooling on the floor below. Jim did not answer except for the answering thrusts of his ass and the pouring out of his passions.

"Fillin' your tank with hot cum, man, and it's runnin' out your prick on the other end! Hot, steamy cum to coat your fuck-cylinder!"

"Hey, Ron, can't you hear me? Turn on the Metro, will ya? I can't leave this right now. Ron, you there? Got to finish up and get out of here. My old lady'll kill me if I don't meet her to shop for shoes for the kids," Jim complained.

Ron shook his head in bewilderment. Jim was still bent over the Caddy's fender, his beckoning ass still stretching the levis invitingly.

"Uh - yeah - OK, just a minute," he answered. He moved to the switch of the machine, his brain slowly clearing. There was a sticky wetness in his crotch.

THE END

CALL OF DUTY

He was gorgeous. Brilliant white Navy uniform, cap on the back of his head so that blond curls tumbled over his forehead, thighs and ass that filled the belled pants to perfection, and a cockbulge that was almost unbelievable. Perhaps most important was the wide but cautious grin on his rugged face when he caught me cruising him in the noisy, smoky bar.

Long Island can be a drag unless you get your kicks from frolicking in the bushes on Fire Island with the ribbon clerks during their holidays from department store basements, or sizzling in the sun at Jones Beach, drooling over the muscles on display. Few people know about the real scene that takes place every year over the July Fourth holiday when a Navy ship pays its respects to a small town on the north shore of Long Island. I don't know how the tradition got started, but I'm in favor.

The ships are usually small, destroyer escorts or minesweepers or some such, but all but a skeleton crew are given liberty, and twenty or thirty randy sailors and a few officers let loose in a small town can transform it in minutes. Of course all the parents lock their virginal daughters behind closed doors for the duration of the weekend; that's good, too, since it leaves all the sailors to us cock-suckers, and the sailors don't really seem to mind, either.

I worked during the summers on the Island and got to know some of the locals including a buddy who lived in that certain small town. Ours was a comfortable relationship, starting out with sex but gradually developing into friendship. Larry had a small apartment (really a loft) that was one big room plus a kitchen and john, and he offered to share the "facilities" with me for the frivolity that might come our way over the holiday. The keys jingled in my pocket as I surveyed the crowded bar that first evening of the holiday.

About half the patrons were sailors, and most of the other half were drooling over the first half. The sailors were complaining to their buddies about the lack of females, but they were on the way to mellowness from the first few beers. They were pretending to ignore the lascivious glances from the gays, but when I shouldered my way to Glenn's side, he didn't complain at all.

"Nice night, eh?" I opened tritely.

"Yeah, sure is. Looks like a nice, quiet little town." His voice was low and non-committal. His eyes searched mine for a moment and then glanced down at the rest of me.

"Gunner's Mate, eh?"

"Yeah, just got a promotion."

"Oh, yeah," I pretended intense interest. "Let me buy you a beer to celebrate."

"Good idea."

He had to act straight, obviously, in front of his buddies, but I knew he was no virgin to the man-to-man scene as soon as we talked for a few minutes. I casually put my foot up on the rail, and he glanced more than once at the bulge extending further and further down my pants leg. His bulge was even more noticeable and he was becoming uncomfortable about it, I could tell.

"There's more beer in the refrigerator at 'my' place", I mentioned when he was close to the bottom of the bottle.

He squirmed and looked away for a moment. "I'm with my buddies, ya know," sort of out of the side of his mouth.

My first thought was "Bring them along!" but I knew better than that. Instead I said, "It's close by. You can be back before they miss you."

"Uh - OK. I'll meet you at the corner in a few

38

minutes."

I had been stood up before and I almost thought this was another such time, but in about five minutes he showed up, a little breathless and looking around to make sure we hadn't been seen. I don't know how he got away from his buddies unless they were also being picked up, which is likely. I hustled him into my car and we drove the few blocks to the apartment. I had lost track of my buddy, Larry, but he could take care of himself!

When we arrived at the apartment he stretched out his incredible frame in a comfortable chair while I went to the refrigerator. When I handed him a beer his hand reached for the bottle and his mouth went to my crotch. He bit gently on the bulge through the pants leg and then nuzzled it with a smooth cheek until it was rock-hard. Even now I go stiff all over again as I think about that handsome sailor face in my crotch, his cap perched on the back of his head, clearly choosing hot cock over the cool beer in his hand.

I took a couple of slugs from my bottle as I watched him, my knees weakening and my heart pounding. This was no time just for a quick blow-job - I wanted him in bed! I stripped off my shirt but he continued to nuzzle, and eventually I had to reach down and pull on his jumper to start him undressing.

"I want that," he murmured as he reluctantly moved back. I helped him out of his jumper and T-shirt, thrilled by the line of blond fur leading from both perky nipples down his broad but lean chest and into his pants.

I moved back out of reach and opened my belt and the top button. Then I stopped, grinning at him. He got the drift. He quickly rose and began to remove the rest, getting the message that this was an all-or-none deal - I wanted skin!

In a flash we were both naked, stiff pricks bobbing at each other, and his was no disappointment. Nine inches of thick, veined cock set off by a warm nest of blond curly hair hiding huge, heavy balls - just as I knew it would be. He wasn't disappointed, either.

His glance shifted from my cock to my face and back again. "You don't know how hungry I get on that fuckin' ship," he confessed. "I think some of the other guys are gay, also, but we are afraid to talk to each other, and don't dare play around at all. Sometimes we watch each other in our bunks, jackin' off in the middle of the night while pretending to sleep. We even play grab-ass in the shower, but pretend it's all a joke."

I stood before him, playing with my eight-incher with one hand and my balls with the other, tantalizing him but tantalizing myself even more. He gripped his cock in a thick fist as he watched me and poured out his frustrations.

"I want to suck that thing, shove it down my throat, and make you shoot a mouthful. I'm not going to swallow it until I have to..."

I couldn't stand any more of this. I moved closer and he took it all in a long gulp just as he promised. I almost shot at that moment but gritted my teeth and pulled back until I could cool off. I grabbed his cap and put it back on his head when he started again, sucking hungrily up and down the shaft and cradling my balls in his free hand. He was jerking himself with the other.

I was afraid he was going to cum that way so I pulled back again. "Let's hit the bed," I said firmly. If he was a one-shot deal I could miss my chance.

He followed me to the bed and I managed to get into a sixty-nine position before he latched on again. His stiff prick in my mouth was sweet and juicy and throbbing with a life of its own. I crammed it down my throat and he took me to the root. We both gurgled happily, gorging ourselves on man-meat, our arms clasped around each other's hips. I switched to his swollen balls and he

40

followed suit, his moist cock riding over my face as I slurped his hairless orbs.

He returned to his first love and I dove down on his prick again, shoving it all the way down my throat. When I came up for air and took it again, I was rewarded with a gush of hot cum that almost strangled me. I couldn't wait and flooded him at the same time, both of us moaning and thrusting and squirting love juice. He tasted sweet and spicy, and I could almost swear I detected a little sea-salt, also.

"Christ," I thought when we tapered off the crest, "it's too soon! He may just want to cut out now when I'm just getting started!"

Wrong. When we finally parted he moved over on top of me and kissed me, hungry as ever. We tasted each other's cum and sparred with our tongues. We were both still hard.

He nibbled on my lips for a while and then started working his way down, tonguing my nipples and then lapping my jerking cock. But I decided it was my turn now. I almost wrestled him to his back and began to really make love to him, biting gently on those pink nipples until he groaned, and then running my tongue along his ridged belly and down to lick his still heavy balls. But I didn't stop there, even though he was tossing his head, wanting to cum again. I had other things in mind.

I began working on his legs, lapping his muscular thighs with their blond fuzz, and then lifted his legs onto my shoulders. His pink asshole winked invitingly at me and tasted as good as it looked. He moaned louder as I circled it and then invaded it wetly. Soon I was able to probe deeply, tasting the very heart of him as he moaned and writhed, clutching the sheet, his eyes shut tight. His thick cock jerked spasmodically against his belly.

41

At that moment I heard a quiet sound at the door and Larry walked in, followed by a young dark man in a Navy officer's uniform! Glenn couldn't see the door even if he could have been disturbed from his fantasy, and apparently he had not heard the door open.

The officer was as brunette as Glenn was blond, but in the dark it would have been a toss-up for beauty. He wore the shoulder boards of a Lieutenant J.G., and my practiced eye judged him to be recently promoted as indicated by the bright sheen to the stripes.

Larry grinned at me, undisturbed. The officer looked distinctly uncomfortable when we saw us, especially me with an inch or two of tongue up the sailor's asshole. But Larry, nonchalant as hell, pulled him along to the side of the bed. The officer looked down and gasped. "Glenn!" he said incredulously.

Glenn's eyes shot open and he stared at the officer. "Sir!" he croaked, and started to struggle away from me. "Mr. Barlow!"

"Glenn, I - " Barlow stammered and then stopped. They stared at each other for several seconds. Then the officer's eyes traveled down the lanky frame, especially embracing the stiff prick that seemed not to have lost its enthusiasm. "You're beautiful," he breathed.

This new development left me speechless, but I guess Larry had been expecting something like this. He started to undress the officer who stood dumbly next to the bed, still staring at Glenn. Gradually their expressions softened to smiles, and by the time Larry had finished the job, they were grinning at each other like Cheshire cats ready to lap up cream.

Larry managed to get Barlow's shoes off and then the pants, releasing a thick, rigid prick that Glenn's eyes locked onto.

"Mr. Barlow," Glenn began, "I always wanted to - I didn't dare - I mean, are you - "

Barlow reached for Glenn's cock and caressed it lovingly. "Just give me a chance and I'll show you, sailor," he said, moving closer.

Glenn beat him to the draw (or the suck). He quickly moved to the side of the bed and slurped in the officer's cock in one gulp. "Ahhh," Barlow breathed, teetering on his toes.

He held Glenn's head almost tenderly in his hands, urging him on. "Yeah, suck it, Glenn, suck it, sailor," he crooned, ignoring both Larry and me entirely. I didn't mind, I had Glenn's cock in my hand and it was stiff and throbbing strongly. Larry was hastily stripping down, anxious to get into the act.

Barlow's muscular thighs began to tremble. It was obvious he was close to climax. Instead he pulled away and leaned down, kissing the sailor deeply. As they kissed he moved to straddle the blond, bringing their cocks to lie side by side, and they went into a muscle-snapping clinch as if they had been starved for this contact for a long time.

I took both cocks in my hand, as much as I could, squeezing them together. Barlow's ass was practically in my face and, never one to miss an opportunity, I began to lick and tongue it. Soon the crisp black hairs in the crease were dripping and his hole was opening to me, although Glenn was his real attraction.

My own cock was demanding attention and that asshole was too inviting to pass up. I moved closer and pressed gently against the dark, moist pucker. Barlow grunted but did not move away. Smearing some more saliva on, I pressed deeper and plugged his ass full. It fit like a glove, a hot clenching glove. It was just as well I had cum only a few minutes before, since I could hold off for a while even though that man-chute stirred my balls immediately.

A nude Larry then knelt at the side of the lovers, his

rampant rod pointing right at their faces. Barlow reached out for Larry and drew him closer. He finally broke the kiss and shoved Larry's cock into Glenn's mouth. Glenn began to feast on hot meat, but his eyes never left Barlow's. I was fucking the officer with long thrusts, and he groaned softly each time I hit bottom.

"Yeah, suck that pretty cock, Glenn - yeah - now watch me suck it - uhmmm - lick those hairy balls - yeah - suck it some more, sailor - "

I continued to jerk the two cocks together as best I could, but I couldn't get my mind off that sailor's sweet ass. Finally I lifted his legs again and managed to get them high enough to get that pretty, pink ass up for service. I changed holes, pushing into Glenn. In this position I could fuck Glenn while I was eating Barlow's ass, and who could ask for anything better?

"Your mouth looks so good full of man cock - lick his ass while I suck him - yeah - ummm - "

Glenn and Barlow were passing Larry's cock back and forth and sometimes licking it together. I don't think Larry cared, but it was obvious to me that they were really making love to each other and Larry was a happy middleman.

"Fuck me - suck it, man - uhhh - uhhh - "

I started to switch holes back and forth, fucking first the sailor and then the officer, and my balls were threatening explosion. My hand was wet with pre-cums from both cocks, and I could tell they weren't going to last much longer, either. One deep plunge into the sailor, then a plunge into Barlow, then back again.

"Yeah, suck it, men," Larry urged, his expression ethereal. Who could blame him, with two hunky navymen almost fighting over his cock? "Oh, Christ, yeah - " Larry moaned. I couldn't take it any more.

I shot long and hard into Glenn - deep in his fiery tunnel, and I guess I yelled my joy because Larry began

44

to shoot almost immediately, too. I jabbed my tongue deep into Barlow's ass as I shot my wad, sort of fucking both asses at the same time. And suddenly my hand was bathed in warm lava from both Glenn and Barlow as they shared Larry's load with loud slurps. It was a four-way cum that blew all our minds.

I let it soak in the sailor for a couple of minutes while I caught my breath, but Larry collapsed on the bed, his cock oozing the last few drops. The navymen returned to their deep kissing, writhing together and smearing Larry's cum all over their faces. Their bellies were slippery from their combined loads, which must have been a real turn-on.

When we all separated eventually, I could see that Glenn was becoming anxious again. We all sat on the bed, sort of staring at each other.

"What do we do now?" Glenn asked, still bewildered.

Barlow gave him a little kiss. "I have been lusting after you for months, ever since I joined the ship, and I'm not going to lose you now," he said firmly. "We are going to get dressed and rejoin the crew as if nothing has happened, but this isn't the last for us."

It sounded like a reasonable solution to me, although maybe a little authoritarian. Maybe that's why Barlow was an officer and Glenn an enlisted man. Anyway, they showered together and were last seen walking back toward the ship in proper uniform, hand in hand. (I wanted to join them in the shower but Larry vetoed the idea, and it was his apartment, after all.)

Then it was my turn to ask, "What do we do now?"

Larry's answer was immediate and incontestable. "Hell, it's still early. We go back to the bar and pick up a couple more sailors! It's our patriotic duty!"

THE END

45

Tight, white sailor uniforms
warrant a salute from any red-
blooded male, even if the action
is mostly between the legs.

BULL TRUCKER

Chuck dropped down the long step from the big rig, a little stiff from long miles of boring highway. He stretched his lanky frame, making his muscles snap and bringing new circulation to his long legs. The truck cab was pretty comfortable, with the air conditioning, cassette player and CB radio, and the bunk behind the seat, but it had been a long ride. With legs as long as his, it took a lot of room to stretch out.

Chuck had recently finished driver's school for the long hauls and had just started his apprenticeship with Roy, a real expert. Roy was also a hell of an attractive guy, but Chuck tried not to think about that. In fact, no one else among the truckers knew he was gay, and he was going to keep it that way, he had firmly decided. Chuck wasn't the brightest guy in the world, but he was sharp enough to know that having the hots for guys was not a good word to get around in the trucker fraternity, or so he assumed.

Frequently during those 800 miles, Roy sort of fondled his dick like he was thinking of balling his old lady, and Chuck would blush and get a start on a hardon, wondering what it would be like to be in Roy's wife's shoes (or on her side of the bed). It hadn't helped, either, when Roy went to sleep on the bunk behind the driver and grew a boner big enough to peak out from under the skimpy blanket. Chuck almost ran the rig off the road when he saw that in the rear view mirror!

But the hardest leg of the trip was over and they were going to stay overnight at a truck stop that night. It was a bustling place, with dozens of trucks parked in the back and a busy coffee shop with bedrooms above for truckers. Chuck stayed with Roy while he gave instructions to the service crew on diesel and service for the truck, and then they had huge helpings of chicken-fried steak, french fries, and apple pie in the restaurant.

One of the waitresses kept making eyes at Chuck until he blushed furiously. Aside from his six foot three inch height and his broad shoulders, Chuck was striking because of his unruly, thick shock of blond hair and deep-set blue eyes that set all the girls fluttering. He also had about the biggest hands and feet of anybody in captivity, but he tried to keep them hidden most of the time to avoid kidding.

Roy had said, when they first met, "You got the biggest feet and hands I ever did see, Chuck. If your cock is as big as them, you got a real problem on your hands."

Chuck wasn't sure what he had meant by that, except maybe it would be too big for most women, but decided to try to keep those appendages out of sight except when needed.

"Yeah, you may not have got too good grades in your written exams, but after seeing you drive, I'd say you got the hang of a big rig," Roy was saying. "By the time we get back home, you oughtta be broken in real well." He chuckled as if with a secret thought. Chuck blinked with questions in his eyes, but Roy merely rose and paid the check.

He handed Chuck one of the keys to the room they would share. "I'm goin' to watch some TV in the lounge and be up to bed later. The room's upstairs any time you want to turn in."

"Guess I'll hit the sack early. Not used to sleeping on that ledge behind the seat yet." Roy smiled. "You'll get used to it, man, you got trucker blood, I can tell." So Roy headed into the lounge and Chuck made his way upstairs.

The room was sparse with twin beds, a cheap dresser, and a toilet without a shower. There was a communal shower down the hall, Chuck had noticed. He decided to sluice some of the grime off. He stripped down, wrapped his towel around his middle, and padded down the hall to the common shower room.

He heard the shower running before he hung his towel on the hook and entered the steamy, tiled room. There were four shower heads, and under one of them, his back turned, was a young Hispanic type with longish black hair. He also had a real trim butt, Chuck automatically noted, but tried to ignore it. No playin' around, he told himself sternly. He adjusted the water temperature in the shower across from the darker man and settled down to relax in the flowing warmth, turned toward the wall with eyes closed to enjoy the water cascading down his back.

"Hi," came a greeting from his shower-mate.

"Hi," Chuck answered noncommittally, not anxious to start a conversation.

"Been drivin' far?"

"'Bout eight hundred miles," Chuck grunted, still not looking around.

"Must get horny, all that way in a bouncin' cab," the man continued, and Chuck's eyes flew open.

"Huh?" he said as he turned to look at the young man for the first time.

He saw a darkly handsome young man, about his own age, with twinkling black eyes and rather thick lips with a trim mustache in between. His body was lean and trim, and at the moment he was holding a very sizable hard cock, all soaped up, in his fist. As Chuck surveyed him, the youth's eyes traveled down the blond's body, over the rounded pecs with their sprinkling of blond, curly hair, the flat, ridged stomach, and the thick bush of light hair at the crotch, to settle on the six inch soft dick swinging freely between his legs. The dark eyes bulged appreciatively.

"Wow! Your partner sure is lucky to be traveling with all that!" he exclaimed, wetting his lips with a pink tongue tip.

"Whadda ya mean?" Chuck tried to growl, but he knew his cock was lengthening and rising even as he pretended not to know what the guy was talking about. The young man continued to milk his dick slowly as he gazed at the blond with hunger in his eyes.

The young trucker was not misled by his show of innocence. He merely grinned and brought his own cock to full attention with his soapy hand. He was going to try to get that before some other trucker snatched him away, he decided.

"What a fuckin' horse cock you got on you," he continued, drawing close. "Don't mind if I touch it, do you?" Without waiting for permission, he grasped the length of it in a soapy hand, and Chuck jerked with the touch.

"How long is that, ten inches or more?" the trucker said wonderingly, stroking it to full staff. Chuck backed up against the wall, torn between loving the touch and fearing the consequences. He guessed he should punch him right there in the shower, but it felt so fuckin' good...

Before he could make up his mind (as I mentioned, Chuck wasn't too quick in the thinking department), the young man knelt and took the still growing head into his mouth, soap suds and all. "Uh," Chuck grunted, knowing that he could not resist a good blow job, even under these circumstances. He stared down at the kneeling worshipper, watching his cock disappear between vermilion lips.

He hit bottom long before it was all in. Eleven inches of thick horse-cock was made for horses, not for human mouths, and there was enough left over for another one or two more guys interested in horny meat. But Chuck was used to that, getting only half way in, and it felt good and hot and satisfying.

"Uhmmm," the Hispanic crooned, trying to stuff more and more down his gullet, then coming up for air, and diving down again until he choked so deliciously. Finally he settled for about half and began to ride up and down, taking as much as he could and tonguing the enormous length with darting slurps.

Chuck's knees started to buckle under the strain. He needed that, he knew, needed a hot mouth taking him, sucking out his cum that otherwise would build up and overflow whenever he slept. That is the way he justified the pleasure of the moment.

"Well, who's your friend, Raul?" came a booming voice at the door. Startled, Chuck looked quickly in that direction, starting to pull away from the hot mouth, but Raul pulled him back, showing no sign of concern.

The newcomer was also Hispanic but older, with silver threads mixed in his thick, black hair. He was shorter, almost chunky but not fat. He sported a thick, handle-bar mustache now curled upward from a wide grin, and began to play with his dick as he watched his buddy driver service the tall, handsome blond.

The cocksucker stopped for a moment. "Get a load of this, Pedro," he suggested breathlessly, holding Chuck's manly meat out for inspection like a prize he had just won in a sideshow. "Eleven inches if not more, and stiff as a fuckin' board," he continued proudly before cramming it down his throat again.

Pedro drew close, fascinated with the action. "Sure is beautiful, Raul. Now do it good like I taught you," he ordered almost in a schoolmaster tone. He started to play with Chuck's nipples as he watched his protege doing his best. He smiled up at the tall blond. "Raul's a good boy, but he's still learning. I'm the expert!"

Chuck wasn't sure he liked the atmosphere that had developed, as if he were a prize bull at auction to the highest bidder - or the best cocksucker, in this case. But the hot mouth tended to drive all such disturbing thoughts from his rather limited brain.

When Raul came up for air again, Pedro took his place. He had been right - he was an expert. In less than a minute he had Chuck standing on tiptoes, his prick straining, aching for release, as the cavernous throat took him to the balls.

Pedro was also wise. He knew better than to maintain that kind of action since the guy would shoot too soon and spoil all the fun. Every couple of minutes, when he felt the young man throbbing dangerously, he pulled back, letting him cool off, only to take it all again in his hot haven. Raul settled down to taking care of Pedro, squatting between them and sucking his buddy's cock as he had apparently done before many times.

Each time he neared his climax it was harder to come down again, Chuck noticed. Every time Pedro pulled back there was more throbbing and jerking of that monster prick before it settled down to quiet nodding, waiting for the next time. He couldn't take much more of this. Pedro decided to change the scene.

"Raul, get up here. I want to see this pretty thing up your ass."

Raul looked up startled. He gazed at Chuck's horse dick in awe and then at Pedro in disbelief.

"Up my ass?" he gasped, staring again at the tool he had tried unsuccessfully to stuff down his throat so recently.

"Yep, come on, soap it up nice now. That's right. Now, back up to it, real slow at first, 'til you get the hang of it," Pedro chuckled.

Chuck didn't resist. It wasn't the first ass he had plugged, but they usually kicked and screamed for a while until they got used to it. The soapy hand started his fires burning again, and so when Raul bent over, spreading his cheeks, he was ready.

Pedro helped position it at the tiny opening with pleasure, his hand barely fitting around the girth. "OK, now, Raul, back up slow and easy - you'll see, it'll slip in just fine," he urged.

Raul pushed back, but there was no way that huge cockhead was going to fit that tiny rosette, try as he might. He gritted his teeth and pushed, and Chuck pushed back, but no progress. Pedro was fondling the huge balls with their soft, light down as he encouraged the strange coupling, and the shower was streaming down on them all. Raul was frantic to take that huge tool up his ass, but it was not in the cards. Finally Pedro had a solution.

"Well, OK, I guess I'm just goin' to have to take it myself! That's too fuckin' good to waste!" He pushed Raul out of the way and settled his own ass in position, pushing back slowly and firmly. As the cockhead spread his muscles and popped through the sphincter, he gave a ragged gasp at the enormity but did not hesitate. Slowly, steadily, he pushed back taking more and more up his bunghole until he thought he would burst.

Chuck's face took on an enraptured expression as the hot ass clenched tightly around the throbbing cockhead and swallowed the shaft with increasing ease. "Yeah," he moaned, his eyes closing, his smile widening as he plumbed the depths of the trucker's ass. Raul watched in fascination and disbelief, almost expecting the stretched asshole to rip at any moment.

And then finally it was in all the way, the down-covered balls pressing against the darker ass, impaling the trucker on his throbbing petard (so to speak).

"Oh, Christ, don't move, man, such a huge prick - so fuckin' hard - so fuckin' deep -" Pedro moaned, but his grimace was gradually being replaced by a grin as his ass adjusted and welcomed the invader.

"Gotta fuck," Chuck moaned, "Gotta fuck your ass!" His balls were in control at that point. To tell him not to move was to expect miracles. And move he did, slowly at first, only half strokes, and then longer and longer, deeper and deeper, his prick driving him to greater and greater strokes up the hot, clasping channel.

"Oh, yeah," he moaned, his muscles bulging and rippling, his ass a pile driver for his engorged prick. There was no stopping now -

"Yeah, fuck 'im, Chuck," a new voice said with a sarcastic ring. Three heads snapped to face Roy who stood leaning naked against the door frame. His face wore a severe expression.

Oh, shit, it's hit the fan, Chuck thought bleakly. With all his good intentions about no sex and playing it straight, and Roy caught him in the act, with two truckers, for Christ's sake! Now he'd never get passed on his driver's training!

They stared at each other for a moment, and then Roy broke up. His face lost his frown and took on a wide grin as he padded naked into the shower, his thick cock swinging and rising at the same time. He placed a hand on Chuck's shoulder in a buddy gesture, but his eyes were fastened on Chuck's cock halfway embedded in the trucker's ass. He fondled the section remaining outside.

"Quite a tool you got there, Chuck. I thought you would. It's a wonder Pedro could take it, but Pedro never was one to give up easy."

"You - know each other?" Chuck gulped.

"Sure we do. My dick's been up there before, too, you know. But right now -" as his hand dropped to Chuck's taut behind, "I got other thoughts in mind." He grinned at his buddy driver as one finger probed his tight asshole.

Chuck grinned back, accepting all at face value. "Guess I owe you," he smiled, and everybody chuckled heartily at the situation.

To cut a long story a little shorter, it wasn't long before Chuck was again balls-deep in Pedro, and Roy was balls-deep in Chuck. Pedro decided he wanted to suck

Raul off while he was getting fucked, and so the foursome made a pretty picture as the shower gushed over their straining bodies.

Raul came first, splattering Pedro's tonsils with pent-up cream in spurt after spurt. He pushed his buddy's head down on his jerking prick, and Pedro gobbled it down like manna from heaven. Raul then scrambled under his buddy and, pushing his flailing fist aside, took his buddy's cock in his mouth with gusto.

All that action and the tight gripping of Chuck's ass brought Roy off next, and he shot wads of joy juice up that tight tunnel. Chuck gloried in the jerking and throbbing of that cock he had admired in the truck. The scratching of the dark, hairy thighs against his and the hairy balls slapping his ass made him forget everything except his own need, and then it happened. Big Vesuvius erupted with a surge of power, the lava flowing freely and hotly, the huge prick thrusting and jerking deep inside the struggling Pedro. This was too much for Pedro, too, and he filled his buddy's throat with streams of cum straight from the balls. They were all in high gear, screaming down the highway at top speed, and there was no stop sign big enough to slow the simultaneous soaring of the randy roadmasters.

Even when it was time to slow down, they continued to thrust and groan but more gently and quieter, their knees quaking, the pricks gradually softening. It was a difficult knot to untangle but eventually the cocks slipped free with reluctance, promising another day.

The four truckers grinned at each other and then silently turned to separate showers, satisfaction plain on their rugged faces. A few minutes later, Roy and Chuck walked slowly down the hall to their room, Roy fondling his buddy's swinging tool that was already showing signs of reawakening.

"You sure passed that test with flying colors," he said grinning. "I might try backing onto that thing myself in the morning..."

THE END

MOON NIGHTS

Rollo floated down the long, convuluted corridor toward the Chief's office at a leisurely pace. As he approached the panel with the crossed lasers, his identity medallion activated the mechanism and the panel hissed open; he was expected. He pressed the button on his wrist control, and the tiny jet on his ankle performed the sharp left turn necessary to send him hovering in front of the ultimate security door.

He didn't really understand why he was hesitating. The Chief was no ogre from Galiptos, after all - just the senior GalaxiFleet commander at this moonstation, the jumping-off point for exploration and maintenance of their assigned segment of the galaxy. Maybe his hover pattern was a holdover from his initial introduction to the Chief who had remarked that he was the youngest Captain in the Fleet; Rollo got the impression that the Commander would be watching him in particular. Or maybe it was what they had called - if his memory of psychohistory was correct - an "inferiority complex" in the twentieth century. Being a brillant student, he had always competed with men several years his senior who at first looked askance at his youth but grudgingly acknowledged his skills as an astronaut and athlete. Irritated by his introspective lapse, he passed his palm over the signal box and was immediately ushered in by a gentle wave of perfumed air.

The secretary/receptionist was a Camaan, and Rollo reacted as he usually did to Camaans - a slight blush followed by a twitch in his contour briefs. This one was especially notable, from the tightly-curled green fuzz on his pointed head at least seven feet above the floor to the two-toed sandals on his feet, not to mention the thick trunk, barely concealed by the uniform tunic, extending nearly two feet upward from his crotch to his rounded chest. Rollo had always wondered what they did in bed - whatever they did it must be spectacular. He also wondered why Camaans were always chosen to work as the private secretaries for Chiefs and other dignitaries...

"You may go in - the Chief is expecting you," he purred through the pursed stoma that passed for a mouth in Camaans. His yellow eyes fixed for a moment on Rollo's crotch which, although not nearly as protuberant as the secretary's, bulged impressively for an Earthling. He waited for a fraction of a moment before pressing the airlock release, looking up at Rollo still a few feet off the floor in horizontal military attitude. Rollo knew the Camaan's vision was acute enough to penetrate the stretched fabric enclosing his cock and balls. "You are looking especially - 'earthy' - today."

Rollo had no time to consider the implications behind that remark, since he was quickly wafted into the office of the Chief of the GalaxiFleet, Fifth Squadron.

"Come on down to earth," the Chief growled as Rollo nearly flew over his head from the abrupt entry the Camaan had energized. The Chief was tethered to his desk which was apparently tied to the floor by transparent strands of colonite.

"Yessir," Rollo responded, doing a neat somersault to bring him down to the Chief's level. He came to rest a few inches off the floor, more or less vertical. He had the almost instinctive earth-taught impulse to salute, but stopped himself in time; a sudden movement of his arm would send him off in another trajectory, and apparently the Chief was in no mood for spatial discussions.

"Captain, I can't tell you yet where your next assignment will be, but I must tell you it may be dangerous and will be an extended tour, several earth weeks, at least."

Rollo inwardly groaned, knowing the stresses that long tours had on his psychic stability. Cooped up for several weeks in a twenty-compartment ship with a group of boring junior officers, some of them female, was enough to leave him scratching the ceiling with frustration. But the Chief was continuing, his stern face suddenly expressionless.

"Because of the duration of the mission, I am going to allow you to pick your own crew from among the volunteers who have already come forward. I must say that, when they were informed that you would be the Captain, there was no shortage of volunteers. Apparently you are, uh - popular with the junior officers and security guards."

His eyes scanned the Captain's lithe, muscular body clearly outlined by the clinging, beige nylex uniform with the magenta-and-gold patch denoting his rank. "Perhaps it is not entirely due to your demonstrated brilliance as a ship's Captain."

"Sir?" Rollo stammered, confused by the Chief's unaccustomed personal insinuations.

"Be that as it may," the Chief continued brusqely and ignoring the question, "it is important that the more personal needs of our crews are satisfied as well as the physical environments we provide for their tasks. I am sure you will agree."

"Oh, yes, sir," Rollo agreed wholeheartedly, beginning to grasp the potentials of the Chief's remarks. "Am I to, uh - interview them and make my choice?"

The Chief nodded. "Use whatever method of selection you prefer. Here are pictures of the qualified volunteers according to their ranks and specialties, in uniform and, uh - without uniform, front and back views. I think you should be able to select a prize crew from this group. You have one week to make your decisions." He handed Rollo a folder of photos, neatly indexed.

Rollo was still considering the implications of his latest assignment when he opened the folder in his stateroom a few minutes later. He decided to nibble on peatein bars rather than join the others in the dining room for dinner while he surveyed the field. He immediately rejected the females, leaving about thirty young men from which to form a crew of twelve. Then he began making a list starting with Navigators.

Carlos from Spanolaxis knew his way around the galaxy but Rollo wasn't turned on by the long foreskin clearly visible in Carlos' picture. Still, the ass wasn't half bad, he mused. Cordan was interesting for an Etruscan and it might be amusing to stick his fingers into the deep hole on each side of his head while experiencing those thick, purple lips... Perhaps it would be better to stick to humans for the majority of the crew, but there were advantages in the capabilities of some of the others. Eventually he selected the top contenders and entered their ID's into the paging computer, assigning fifteen minutes for each in series. That should be enough to perform an initial screening, he thought. Along with his other duties, it should be possible to interview four or five each day to reach a final decision in the one week allotted. He set his door release to open automatically for each at their appointed times.

At the precise time, the first candidate, Phil, hissed through the panel. Rollo's first reaction was that he was out of uniform, since he wore only a heavy black leather codpiece, leather boots, a leather harness around his almost hairless chest, and a leather helmet which nearly concealed his blond curls. He was certainly an excellent specimen of human. His codpiece was of necessity very large, extending at least ten inches out and down as befitted his equipment. The aroma of leather and all its sensual implications filled the compartment.

"You know why you're here?" Rollo asked to conceal his initial shiver of appreciation for the navigator's beauty in his unusual garb.

"I think so, sir," was the soft-spoken reply. "I just received your computer summons a couple of minutes ago, and there was no choice but to come as I am." He blushed becomingly, glancing down at his attire.

Rollo's contour briefs began to reshape around his elongation. "That is exactly what I had in mind, for you to come as you are."

"Sir?" Phil inquired uncertainly. Rollo did not elaborate.

"Come here," Rollo ordered, pointing to the space above his head. With a tap of a foot on the floor, Phil jetted to the assigned station and Rollo arrested his movement by grasping the huge codpiece, his main interest.

From the spongy consistency of the leather sheath it was obvious there was more to come. The delicate aroma of leather and human male crotch stirred Rollo's desires, reminding him of the ancient and universal fascination of this combination throughout the galaxy's history. And when he tugged him close to taste and nibble on the leather encasement, his own briefs snapped their moorings as programmed to allow for more important functions.

As Rollo had hoped, the codpiece began to swell and buckle, pulling tightly against the thin leather strap extending up the crack of his ass. The harder his jaws clamped down, the more distorted the codpiece became and the taller his own cock grew between his legs. The taste of the leather was aphrodisiacal as lovers had found since Cromagnon times.

"Arggg," Phil breathed, and Rollo interpreted this as an indication of pain, an understandable effect of the restriction. He discovered a concealed connector at the base of the codpiece and snapped it open. Along with a sigh from Phil there was an abrupt catapulting of the codpiece outward with the force of the huge, blood-congested prick it contained. Another twist of a quick-release mechanism and the entire organ was revealed it all its delectable glory. Rollo maintained his grasp of the now empty codpiece to keep the navigator from drifting away.

The eight-centimeter thick column was precisely straight and light pink in color. Although of course there was no foreskin (that unnecessary appendage having disappeared during recent earth evolution), the darker pink head was swollen to the size of a tree-grown orange and carried on its velvet surface a redolence of the leather that had encased it. Rollo gazed at the imposing tool fully thirty centimeters in length, and felt certain that this could occupy many of the slack hours on a long space voyage.

Huge, globular balls nestled snuggly at its base, each bearing silky down to match the pubic hair curled seductively to set off the proud display. The sight that met the Captain's eyes more resembled a golden horse in leather harness than a human.

The time was passed for admiration - Rollo stretched his lips around the bulbous cockhead while maintaining his grasp on the shaft. It tasted sweet and a little fruity, like a fine wine made from white grapes in the old fashioned way, with the additional, subtle taste of leather that inflamed him so mysteriously. As his tongue caressed the smooth surface, the head swelled even more in reward for his efforts, and Phil emitted a strangling sound which Rollo interpreted as an appreciative moan.

As Rollo attempted to take more of that giant phallus, he nearly strangled himself. Even with one hand around the shaft, he still could not take all of the remainder in his mouth and throat. He found that by sucking up and down repeatedly he could accommodate more and more of it, a challenge he accepted without hesitation.

He recalled the lush allure of the navigator's ass as pictured in the photos the Chief had provided. He decided to make use of that, since there was some difficulty in maintaining the navigator's position above him in space.

His fingertips drifted backwards and up the tantalizing crease of the ass until they encountered the pink pucker he sought. Inserting one finger into that passion portal allowed him to tether his candidate to the site of the action, as well as send another surge of anticipation through his already throbbing cock.

He was content, for the moment, to suck more and more of that beautiful prick into his throat and caress the hot, clinging tunnel beckoning behind. With his freed hand he was able to grasp and roll the golden balls in his fingers. Phil trembled in the hands of his superior, and his legs began a swimming movement set up by the triple stimulation. Their simultaneous moans were the only sounds in the climate-controlled compartment.

At the moment Rollo thought he had finally thrust the huge cockhead fully into his throat, his door panel hissed open, admitting the next applicant. His first interview had taken longer than he had anticipated. Rollo stared around his engrossing task at Semelin, a young navigator from Mensin, one of the smaller galaxies. Although properly dressed in the uniform of the day, his incredibly broad shoulders, trim ass, and thick legs characteristic of the Mensins seemed to Rollo's feverish brain vaguely to resemble the classic satyr of ancient Greek mythology. This was further emphasised by the huge bulge at his crotch and extending down one leg.

Semelin looked startled at the sight that met his eyes, but this could only be detected by a slight flaring of his tubular mouthparts. If he had had eyebrows above his brilliant green eyes, they probably would have arched sharply.

"Uh, sorry - am I early, sir?" Semelin inquired, his gaze flicking back and forth between Rollo's face between the legs of the navigator and his crotch sporting the un-touched prick.

Rollo thought quickly. He did not want to relinquish

63

his prize possession, and the situation could be informative as interview material. He ignored the question, returning to his task with gusto. Semelin passed the subtle interview test with flying colors. After only a few seconds of hesitation, he projected himself to a kneeling position between Rollo's knees and began to suction his stiff cock into his deep oral cavern with alacrity.

"Suction" is the proper word. The Mensin mouthparts are tubular because they have always survived on liquid nutrients formed in springs and lakes on their planet. Dozens of tiny tongues lined these muscular tubules, and Semelin put them to work hungrily on the Captain's cock. The result was an agonizingly delirious sensation of fluttering and siphoning of life juices that brought tingles and rumbles from his balls as no human mouth had ever done.

"Uggh", he gurgled, mouth full of juicy, human cock that even then was beginning to jerk and throb in anticipation. Rollo pushed in a second finger along side the first in the spasming ass above him, and was rewarded by the snapping of Phil's powerful leg muscles, rigid in preparation for the ultimate release. Rollo had the fleeting impression of being sandwiched between two horses, the golden stud above and the alien stallion below, a team bent on bearing him to heaven beyond the known galaxies. His balls were already rumbling, warming up for a blast-off.

Phil's first spurt of heady cum set off the cascade. With the second spurt Rollo's juices exploded in the Mensin's mouth channel, all the internal tongues coordinating in milking every drop from the human's prong. Rollo's mouth was quickly filled to overflowing with the sweet cum, and despite rapid swallowing, some drops escaped to float freely in the rarefied air. They formed a faint halo around the Captain's head even as his balls emptied themselves to feed the Mensin. The suction was so intense that it seemed his reservoirs were completely emptying under the negative pressure.

Although the crest of the wave seemed to last for an eternity it was over all too soon. Rollo struggled to swallow the remaining ooze tapering off as his own release slowed, and he eased his fingers from Phil's ass. This set the navigator free, and his cock reluctantly left its warm haven to float away while Phil caught his breath. Semelin continued to try for more of that bubbling brew until Rollo eased him away; the sensation was too intense.

"Umm," Semelin smacked. "High protein." It was not possible to tell whether or not he was smiling.

Phil came to stand trembling alongside the Captain, attempting to achieve an attention stance, and Semelin rose to his feet, not sure what to expect. That brought the eyes of both humans to the huge erection extending down inside the leg of the Mensin's uniform. The clinging nylex was being stretched beyond its intended bursting point. With one accord they reached for it and Semelin was only too happy to release it from its confines.

The horse analogy persisted. Both Rollo and the navigator knelt, one on each side, to do homage to the forty centimeter prick that thrust from that equine crotch, their mouths and tongues tracing the enormous length and lapping the huge, bulbous, vermillion head that promised even more ecstasies. The taste of honey and cinnamon greeted their tongues.

At that moment the door panel hissed open admitting the next candidate. It was Methos, the black Gorgian whose faint green patina and spectacular round ass had reminded Rollo of an after-dinner mint which only whetted the appetite. He also had some ideas about the Gorgian's twenty centimeter tongue that could be unfurled from his silver-furred face.

It should be an interesting intergalactic voyage. It also promised to be a long, wonderful night.

THE END

THE BEST KIND

WANTED Real man to take me in hand
and show me by his actions what I
should do to really satisfy him.
Call Steve anytime at 555-6969.
Hurry! I'm hurting!

I sat and stared for a couple of minutes at the advertisement I had drafted. Was it too much, too obvious?
Would the admission of my frustration turn a prospect
on or off? Maybe yes, maybe no, I decided. Would it
attract kooks rather than real men? Maybe, but would
that be so bad? At least it was honest. That's the way
I really felt those days.

Well, it might bring the weirdos out, but almost
anything would be better than what I had now, I decided,
as I quickly stuck the sheet of paper in an envelope. I had
addressed the envelope days ago to one of the local gay
rags but hadn't built up the nerve until that day to really
go through with it, really write the confessions of my
tormented soul to whomever it might concern. I put a
stamp on it and placed it carefully on the shelf near the
door so I wouldn't forget to mail it the first time I went
out.

I turned to the mirror by the door and surveyed myself
critically. Five feet, ten inches (average), brown, curly
hair (average), brown eyes with flecks of green (quite
average, really), pretty broad shoulders and slim waist but
nothing special (average), a mustache that needed
trimming and looked a little shorter on the right than the
left, kind of thick lips but nothing special (did they really
appear "kissable"?), and a few wisps of curly brown hair
visible through my shirt neck (average). I turned to the

side and appraised my ass in the faded jeans. Not bad, really, not flat but not really exactly rounded like some of those guys who preferred the short shorts and running shoes. My legs were good, I guessed, maybe from all the tennis I had played since age 10, fifteen years ago. But only my dull tennis partners saw them bare these days. And my cock was pretty good, too (maybe a little bit better than average), but only my hand knew the truth these days. Was I already over the hill at twenty-five?

I had lots of friends, good friends, too, but one doesn't have sex with his friends. Mike often breezed in on his way to the beach or some other cruisy spot, inviting me along, but I rarely went. It usually turned out that I would watch Mike cruise and even make out with some hunk with only half a brain, and I would just envy him and go home alone.

Joe was always friendly but had a so-called lover who monopolized his time, although they hadn't had sex in years, or so Joe said. Still they remained together, and I wondered exactly why. Joe told me he masturbated every night while taking his shower.

Brian stalked the all night movie houses and made out with God knows what kinds of diverse creatures in the dust and candy wrappers (or so I imagined), even though he was a really attractive guy who could probably have anybody he chose. For Brian it seemed it had to be strange and anonymous to be enjoyable.

The oppressive silence of the apartment, except for the muffled street noises outside, grated my nerves and I settled in front of the TV. I flipped through the channels but couldn't decide between a nature story about llamas and a sit-com about some silly high school girl. Impatiently I switched it off and went down the street to the corner pub, remembering to drop my advertisement in the mail box on the way. Some glances were directed at me, but when I made no positive response they drifted away. No one seemed to interest me, or if they did, there was something wrong somehow. After listening for an hour to the same hyped up rock and the babble of familiar voices, I returned home and went to bed.

For the next week I hurried home after work and stayed close to the phone. The few times it rang it was only Joe complaining about his "lover's" indifference, or Brian regaling me with the latest sex episode in a theater balcony, or an insurance salesman with a tired voice who had picked my name out of the phone book at random to present his pitch. No response to my ad. But then I realized that it probably would not be published until the next week. By that time I might be too old to care!

Finally I stripped down and looked at myself in the full length mirror. Would I be interested if I came across the image before me? Damned if I knew. My cock was hanging well below twin balls gorged with juice, and as I stroked it absently-mindedly, it grew in my fist. What the hell, I groaned, and took advantage of it. I jerked furiously, snarling at my reflection, and within a very short time there was an obscene, milky trail dribbling slowly down the glass. But there was no thrill to that.

By the middle of the next week, I had practically forgotten sending in the ad. I started rereading some gay fiction and refused an offer from Mike to spend the weekend in the mountains. I decided I was the hermit type, after all.

As was my habit on Friday night, I tried to break the spell by going to a leather bar in the warehouse district. I had to park several blocks away, but the walk to the bar was worth it if no more than to smell the leather-swathed dudes and to fantasize on what it would be like to bed down with one of them. It never happened, of course, but it made a nice dream. I was already part way into such a fantasy as I walked by the opening of an alley - and was snatched into the darkness by a muscular leather arm!

"Hey! What - " I started, before a heavy hand was clamped over my mouth.

"Shut up, man, or you'll get more than you bargained for!" a gruff, raspy voice snarled. It was so dark that I could see little except a looming shadow in black leather with tiny glimmers of light reflecting from studs and chains.

"Down on your knees, slave!" The order was undeniable, and the steel in the arms pinning me to the wall was enforcement enough. Slowly I sank to my knees, my head spinning, and felt a packed leather crotch press against my face.

"You'd like to suck that prick, wouldn't you, man." It wasn't a question but an assumption of fact, and I didn't even bother to answer. There wasn't much time anyway, since the long, thick tube was extracted and a hot, flaring cockhead was meeting my lips.

"Suck it - suck it!" the gruff voice became sibilant and insistent, and I opened my mouth to feel the stiff cock probe deeply, trailing sweet pre-cum over my tongue. I was abruptly reminded of how good a stiff cock was, how much it filled my mouth, and how satisfied my throat could feel as it welcomed a hefty hardon. Deeply, deeply it thrust, and I greeted the near suffocation with happy acceptance, my head shoved painfully against the brick wall behind me.

"Ahhh," I heard my assailant moan as his cock throbbed in my throat. Then he pulled out almost all the way and shoved in again, all the way to the balls that pressed against my quivering chin. The cock seemed to swell even more, and when the man began to pump, fucking my face with controlled but maximal thrusts, I sagged against the wall, wanting more and more, taking all I could get. My wrists had been released, and I clutched the leather boots like life preservers as I serviced the unknown stud.

"You need that fuckin' dick, don't ya, man," that gruff voice taunted, and I could only nod in assent, feeling my own prick strain stiffly against my levis. "You want to swallow a man's load, don't ya, man," the voice continued, and again I nodded in agreement, my brain shouting it loud and clear. "Do I!" I thought, struggling to handle all that precious meat that was strangling me so enjoyably.

"Well, take it then, cocksucker!" the man rasped, and pistoned twice more before spurting cream thick and sweet, rich and potent into my mouth and down my throat. I gulped and gurgled, the heady load coating my tonsils and cascading down my throat. God, it was good! My own cock twitched alarmingly, oozing pre-cum to soak my levis, but didn't actually lose any of its urgency.

The man continued to thrust in and out, his initial insistence tapering off as his orgasm passed, until the softening shaft lay quietly on my tongue. I held a mouthful in my mouth, the taste and texture exhilarating after all that time of famine, and finally reluctantly let it go down. I heard a sigh and another sound, almost a chuckle, before the cock was withdrawn and stuffed back into the leather crotch. I remained on my knees, catching my breath, relishing the taste of man and his precious juices. I stared up toward the face, but still could not make out the features, only the leather cap with the steel rim around the brim.

As abruptly as we had met, the man quickly stalked out of the alley and was gone. I still knelt in the filth of the alley, staring after him. I was trembling with reawakened lust superimposed on the fear from the sudden abduction. After weeks of nothing, the experience had been earth-shattering! My cock still jerked frantically, wanting, needing more!

Stiffly I finally struggled to my feet and made my way back to the car. My assailant was nowhere to be seen.

I forgot my intention of visiting the bar and made my way home, still trembling. I collapsed in a soft chair staring at nothing, reliving the brief moments of ecstacy in the blackness of the alley. The phone rang.

The hand that lifted the receiver was shaky. My voice quivered "Hello?", and - nothing. Just silence. A person breathing, deep breaths for several seconds, and then "click" as the receiver was replaced. "Hello? Hello!" I repeated, but only the dial tone answered. I sagged back into the chair. A wrong number at this time of night! I contemplated the damp spot in my crotch, now cool and sticky.

A few minutes later there was a knock at the door. Probably the straight couple in the next apartment needing another bottle of scotch, I thought. I had heard sounds of a party when I passed their apartment door on the way in. As I opened the door I noticed that the hallway lights were out. A dark figure stood just around the door frame, a mask covering part of his face, but the extended hand held a gun.

"Don't say or do anything. Just turn around and face into the apartment." The voice was masculine but a hoarse whisper, and I stiffened at the obvious threat. I stared at the gun which did not waver. "Turn around!" the voice again ordered, and I had no choice but to obey.

The figure came close to my back, the gun pressing between my shoulder blades. "Now walk - slowly - into the bedroom." My knees began to weaken. God knows what I was in for now! The damn city was overrun with thieves and housebreakers! I might be killed if I didn't do as I was told! My money, what there was, was in my wallet in clear view on the dresser, I thought.

I was almost to the bedroom door before I thought, "Why didn't I try to get a peek at this goon as I passed the mirror in the hall?" Too scared, too startled. The man remained close behind me, the gun continuing to press authoritatively.

"Don't turn the light on." The man could see that the bedroom was dark and apparently wanted it that way. I walked in slowly, the man close behind, until I reached the bed. I heard the door close behind us.

"Now take off your clothes."

That order was perhaps the most startling of all. Probably it was to prevent my following the burglar after the dirty deed was done? If I was able to follow after the man was finished with me!

"Take 'em off, now!" The gun pressed harder, almost drilling a hole between my shoulder blades. I hastened to comply, the pressure of the gun following at each stage of undressing. Soon I was nude except for my socks.

"On your knees by the bed, faggot!" Faggot? What's that got to do with it, I asked myself silently. But I did as I was told. "Now lie flat on the bed on your belly and put your hands behind you."

Oh, oh, he was going to tie me up. What a fuckin' predicament this was! "Give me your hands!" the voice ordered huskily. I complied, and immediately felt the steel bite of handcuffs placed around both wrists!

"Hey!" I began, my first spoken response in the entire scene so far, but I didn't get far. "Shut up, faggot!" the voice rasped. The pressure of the gun barrel was gone, but instead there was an iron fist controlling my manacled wrists. Another hand gripped one of my ass cheeks possessively.

"Hmm, not bad," the character whispered hoarsely. The other cheek was pinched also, a thumb coming to rest on my asshole. Then fingertips drifted across the tense opening, back and forth, back and forth hypnotically, and my nervous state was further complicated by an unconscious reaction of desire despite my desperate situation. I squirmed and wriggled, my cock stiffening.

The fingertips were removed and replaced by

73

something smooth and moist, circling the anxious bunghole and then probing the opening. The hot tongue dipped and darted, lapping lasciviously and languorously, then more determinedly, demanding entrance. The quivering in my body was due to a mixture of fear and longing. The forbidding figure was reducing me to a puddle of mush, a groveling slave. I felt the tongue entering me deeper and deeper, and knew that I would be unable to fight off any onslaught if it continued. I was not aware that I moaned and pressed back to have as much as I could.

But then the tongue was replaced by a firm, warm object, and I felt a thick cockhead beginning its invasion. It had been so long since a thick prick had touched my asshole, I wondered if I could take it. But the man advanced slowly, his spit lubricating as it went, and soon all I could think of was "More! More!" My face was buried in the bedspread, my eyes closed in expectant joy, as the rod was pressed further and deeper into my welcoming tunnel of love.

After what seemed like an eternity, an eon of increasing fullness and excitement, I felt hairy balls press against me and knew I had it all. Whoever this creep was, he had a fuckin' big prick, no doubt about that, I thought. It felt so good up my bunghole, empty for so long. And as the man began to move in and out, I felt myself opening more and more, taking the huge, hot muscle deep in my gut.

"You need to be fucked, don't ya, man," the hoarse whisper came from the gloom behind me. "Big dick up your twitchy little ass, huh?" Yeah, the bigger the better... "You let a man know what you want and he'll give it to ya," came the somewhat mysterious advice punctuated with heavy thrusts of the plunging prick.

My cock was trapped against the side of the bed, and it was dribbling its response to the prostate massage going on inside. I wanted to grip it, caress it, make it speak its own message for the joy the man was bringing, but I could not. The handcuffs marred the wrists as I pulled against the immobilization, but to no avail. The burglar had me apparently exactly where he wanted, on my knees, unable to ward off the inevitable, taking his passion when and where he wanted. And I had to admit to myself that I wanted exactly what he was giving me, and in the way I wanted to get it.

I felt my attacker grip my balls and cock between my legs as he continued to plug my hole mercilessly. The rough hand brought me close to the point of eruption, especially the tight constriction and the feeling of submission to the stranger. My balls felt tense, full to overflowing, but there was no relief in sight. The lunging lance proceeded to plunder and pillage in the most enjoyable of ways.

It couldn't last forever, of course. I could hear the man's breathing become ragged and his plunges became more desperate. I struggled to meet each plunge, wanting and needing the ultimate invasion, until the groans of my attacker became louder and louder, ending in a low scream of unbridled joy and triumph. The huge ramrod began to twitch and jerk deep in my gut, and the grip around my jewels grew excruciating.

"Uh - uh - uh," the man panted, spurting deep into my hot ass, filling his victim with boiling lava straight from his balls. I was forced face down by the man's heaviness against me, the weight pressing me into the mattress as he gave his all. I knew my ass was circling, urging the man on to greater and greater efforts, clenching and clamoring for all I could get.

Gradually his actions became calmer, the storm passing. I could hear the man panting, trembling from the peaking exertion his body had dictated, and I could feel the cock shrinking slowly, its major task completed.

Slowly the man retreated and the prick slipped out, my ass obligingly permissive and perhaps satiated for the moment. I hadn't felt so good in a long time, and it had been a long time since my last good fuck. I did not move, preferring to relish the moment and the surrender that had been mine.

I heard the adjustment of clothing behind me, and thought the man rose to his feet. Suddenly my wrists were released from their bonds and I gradually stirred. I turned then, only to catch a glimpse of a dark figure hurrying out the door, and a moment later I heard the apartment door close behind him.

Stunned and confused, I remained on the floor for a moment and then dragged myself up on the bed and lay there panting, my cock stretching toward the ceiling. What kind of a burglar forces his way in the door and contents himself with giving the greatest fuck of his life to his victim, then leaves without taking anything? And the leatherman in the alley; he could have taken anything he wanted, but was content with getting his rocks off - and so gloriously! - in my mouth? What the fuck?

After a few moments of confusion, I dragged myself into the shower and sluiced down, soaping my still rampant cock and my used but happy asshole with more pleasure than I had for weeks. I had just reached for the towel when the doorbell rang. Still dazed I padded to the door with the towel around me, and opened it to - a drag queen in a long, silver gown and huge, floppy hat in the best Scarlet O'Hara tradition!

"Hi, big boy, I understand you need to be shown what to do for a man! Well, I'm here to show you!" she lisped in the worst southern-belle accent I had ever heard. "Honey, I've had more men that I can count, and I'm here to give you all the advice you'll ever need!"

"Brian!" I gasped, seeing through the mascara and false eyelashes immediately.

"A man needs to know you want him, honey, and then it's no holds - and holes - barred!" The queen fluttered the long eyelashes seductively.

"What the fuck are you talking about -" I started, but just then, appearing on either side of Brian were the leatherman, Mike, leather gleaming and studs glistening, and the burglar, Joe, who was just lifting his mask.

I gasped, suddenly realizing what had happened that night. I dropped the towel around my feet in astonishment as my friends crowded into the apartment around me.

"Don't you know what trouble you could get in, advertising that way, you idiot?" Mike demanded, his eyes and fist drawn to the semihard cock in my crotch.

"Yeah, you asshole, we saw your ad in the paper with your familiar phone number, and decided to teach you a lesson, a really pleasant lesson, I might add. But I could have robbed you blind as well as fuck your ass," Joe added, his hand caressing the part he had recently "plundered".

Brian was stripping off his eyelashes, the silver gown, and the floppy hat, his hairy chest and enticing crotch coming into view. "Yeah, but instead we'll all here, and we're all buddies, only now we're fuck buddies, the best kind!"

I grinned widely, my eyes sparkling, vistas suddenly opening up. "Yeah! Why didn't we ever do this before? Sure! Fuck buddies! So let's fuck!"

THE END

A good friend is even a
better friend if he has
a nice cock and a
fuckable ass.

SAKURA AND SAYONARA

He was a beautiful man. Taller than most of his race, he glided gracefully to the next table, his eyes meeting mine for an instant but distracted by the waiter. His trim body in the western suit, his sensitive face carefully expressionless, his black eyes twinkling as if ready to smile with a word of greeting, took me back many years to my first visit to Japan...

I was attending an international conference, one of the first to be held in Japan after the close of World War II, and there had been very little time to explore Tokyo which was still recovering from the war's devastation. To tell the truth I had never thought much about Japanese men as sex objects until those few days when the occasional native caught my eye and roused my desires. The meeting had kept me busy night and day, but on my last night in Tokyo I was determined to find out more than the few words I had learned in the hotel.

A friend who had returned recently from Japan had scribbled some names and vague addresses of some spots he thought would interest me. Unfortunately, I found, the phonetic spelling of the names of the bars had no counterpart on the buildings, and even the streets that wandered seemingly aimlessly between shops giving forth pungent odors of teriyaki and ginger and fish could not be relied on to keep the same name for more than a few blocks.

I towered over the Japanese pedestrians uncomfortably as I strolled uncertainly through the messy streets. There were some in western attire, but most of the adults were wearing casual kimonos and wooden *geta* on their feet. A few women in bright silk and embroidered kimonos hurried by, probably bound for work in some of the entertainment spots that blasted American music into the streets. I sometimes felt the eyes of the women and also some of the men, but when I turned my head to meet them they were always downcast politely.

I'm still not sure how I found the place except that it was on a corner and I noticed an American serviceman leaving as I approached. Weary of the search, I decided to give it a try, even if it was not one of the places on my friend's list. I stooped to enter under the *noren* flapping in the breeze, and was immediately greeted with the friendly odor of beer and scratchy phonograph sounds of American music several years old.

There was a small bar on the left and even smaller tables on the right and disappearing in deepening darkness toward the rear. Contrary to my experience on the street, every eye seemed to meet mine as I stood uncertainly at the door, feeling huge and ungainly in the tiny spotlight over my head. Everyone there was at least a foot shorter, but they were all males except for a slight figure in an orange silk kimono who fluttered to my side, apparently the "hostess". Her face was painted white in geisha style, and her eye makeup was perfection. She tugged on my sleeve to lead me to the back, showing me a tiny table and a low bench which accommodated my six feet muscular frame with some difficulty. She murmured something and I caught the word "whisky", and I nodded. In a minute there was a glass of pungent brew and a bottle of soda water in front of me, and she left with a quick bow and a charming smile.

Now that my entrance had been accomplished, I no longer was the obvious center of attraction, but as my eyes grew accustomed to the darkness I caught gleams from several of the boys in casual discussions with their friends; they all seemed to know each other very well. They were all dressed similarly in white shirts and tight black pants, and as they moved around the bar, talking and joking briefly with their friends, their taut butts

80

stirred the lascivious in me. I was still content to take in the scenery and absorb the unfamiliar when one of the boys detached himself from his group and approached me flirtatiously. I had the distinct impression that his friends had dared him to talk to the tall American who sat all alone in the darkness.

"Konichiwa", he smiled like a Madonna, his black eyes twinkling mischievously under incredibly long lashes. "You are American?" His voice was soft and gentle, but the shirt open almost to his navel revealed a solid, hairless body with the finely etched muscular definition of a tiny man. His smoky skin caught flickering highlights from the colored lights from the bar and contrasted enticingly with the white shirt and gleaming teeth.

"Yes", I smiled back, immediately entranced and also relieved that he spoke English. "My name is Bill."

His smile faded as he attempted the word. "Bil-u?" He looked anxious about getting it right.

I smiled back and nodded. "Close enough. What is your name?" I asked slowly and precisely. He told me what it was but I could not be sure what he said.

"May I join you?" he asked politely.

"Yes, of course," I answered, moving over on the bench.

His smile broadened and his eyes regained their mischief. Instead of seating himself on the bench he plopped himself in my lap, laughing up at me coquettishly. If he had been an American in a bar back home I probably would have resented the familiarity, but instead I laughed and settled his tiny butt right where it belonged. I felt my cock lurch at the hot, rounded touch, and he probably did also.

At this short distance, his face was flawless and without beard except for a few crisp hairs above his lips. Although the signs were extremely subtle, I could discern almost every thought that crossed his mind, I believed,

81

by the fleeting line that could appear between his eyes or a momentary twitch around the mouth when he was amused. His eyes spoke directly to mine, although their directness was almost unnerving.

"You like me?" he asked unnecessarily. I hesitated, because it might be a prelude to a hustle, I thought, and he sensed the hesitation immediately.

"Perhaps you like traditional boy better?" I was surprised to hear the sophisticated word and did not answer immediately. He apparently interpreted my hesitation as agreement, and hurriedly squirmed off my lap. "You wait - I come back," and disappeared behind a curtain in the rear wall.

It was obvious that everyone in the bar had followed this episode with rapt attention, but they pretended total involvement in discussions with their friends. The music had changed to Japanese, and the soft strains of "Cherry Blossoms" on the *koto* and flute replaced the harsh jazz. The hostess brought me another glass of whisky and then suddenly the boy was back, dressed in a white cotton kimono with some insignia etched on it. He bounced back in my lap with a tiny giggle, and this time the contact was even warmer. I realized that he had nothing on under the kimono and it was his bare ass that now warmed my American gabardines. He drew the kimono around him like a skirt and bounced a little, giving my cock additional trouble in control.

After a quick glance into my eyes he lay his head on my shoulder, and I found myself wrapping my arms around his tiny body that seemed to fit so well. He wriggled his ass and my cock stood hard and throbbing, but my mood was strangely quiet, reacting to his loving admiration with almost fatherly calm. His face showed his contentment.

He only remained a moment on my shoulder, but straightened up and held my whisky to my lips. I sipped as we looked into each other's eyes, and then I held the glass for him to drink. He took only a drop out of politeness, I sensed. My rigidity was becoming uncomfortable in confinement, and I shifted slightly.

"I sorry I give you pain. Let me fix." Quickly his hands moved under his kimono and I felt my fly being opened. In a few seconds I was free, rearing strongly between his warm buns. His eyes grew wide and almost round, apparently startled.

"Oh, so big," he murmured and again lay his head on my shoulder as he squeezed it gently between his legs. "I want make you happy," he whispered in my ear. He drew back to look into my eyes, and saw only growing excitement and involvement, an overwhelming fascination with this new, living toy of a boy.

Without discussion he rose on his haunches and I felt him move my cockhead to his tiny opening. It kissed me hotly, but the difference in sizes made any advance very questionable. I am no slouch for a six-foot Caucasian, and it was almost surely the largest one he had ever encountered.

He bore down on the vertical cock and it started to enter. I watched his face closely because I didn't want to hurt him. At first there was a line of determination around the mouth which changed to slight crinkles at the corners of his eyes as his ass was spread unnaturally. The heat clasping me brought even more swelling and did nothing to ease the task, but he determinedly moved slightly up and down, teasing himself open gradually. His eyes were suddenly moist from what must have been genuine pain. I tried to relax but that was impossible. My pulse was racing and my legs began to tremble as the invasion of his most intimate aperture continued under his control.

The others in the bar had not paid particular attention to us when he was sitting on my lap, but I sensed now that everyone in the bar knew exactly what was occurring. The glances sent our way were fleeting but knowledgeable and perhaps slightly disapproving, but I didn't care. I was being engulfed by a near virgin in full view, and my rapture was probably apparent to all.

Finally, impossibly, he was seated squarely on my lap again, my cock filling him, and as he moved I could actually feel its mass as I held him closely around his waist. His eyes were round; the tears were gone, replaced by a wonderment and a fulfillment which was thrilling to both of us. And as he moved in small circles the clasping heat set my teeth on edge with desire. Any other time my tendency would be to thrust and grind, but with this boy I was content for the moment to let nature take its course.

I suddenly became aware that the hostess was beside me again. "Please excuse boy, sir. He is student and much enthusiastic." I am sure my face revealed my dazed fascination, and I could only smile weakly.

The boy showed his contentment by again raising my glass to my lips as the hostess watched, and when I had gulped a swallow he set it down and began to raise and lower himself. I gasped with the exquisite pleasure he brought me, his tight ass milking my cock and his handsome face glowing with pride and adoration for me. Gradually he increased his pace, and I heard a muffled grunt from the hostess still watching closely.

The room faded from my vision. For the moment we two were the only ones in existence. I worked one hand under his kimono skirt and encountered a very rigid cock between his legs, throbbing strongly to my touch. The size was consistent with the rest of him but certainly not tiny - I had stroked smaller ones on much taller Caucasians. I gripped it tensely and was rewarded by a gasp of pleasure even as he continued his ministrations. His face was flushed with his effort and the joy I was apparently bringing him.

My elbow brushed the stiff material of the hostess' kimono, and I turned toward her blankly. From between cleverly disguised folds in the material protruded a respectably-sized stiff cock only inches away from my face. I looked up startled, and realized for the first time that the "hostess" was in drag. My face must have mirrored my confusion, but I was in no position to be concerned about appearances at that moment. My balls were signalling their intense need, and the boy's cock dripped its warning moisture over my hand.

I quickly pulled the "hostess" closer and gobbled in that twitching cock, burying my nose in the stiff fabric of the kimono. The prick filling my mouth, already moist from pre-cum, added another dimension to the ecstatic coupling, and I seemed to float high and anchorless in a sea of lust.

The boy's breathless efforts grew more and more demanding, and I knew I could tolerate the pressure no longer. Once, twice, I thrust up hard, skewering the boy massively before I shot long and hard, deep into his silken cavern. He gasped and answered my volley with one of his own, flooding my hand with rich cream in spurts matching mine. I moaned and grunted, and was rewarded with a sweet tide of manjuice from the "hostess" now firmly embedded in my throat. We soared heavenward in a parabola of passion, oblivious to the curious eyes and sounds in that little corner of Tokyo.

* * * * * * * * *

I don't really remember much after that. I know the boy disappeared and the hostess was soon attending "her" customers again, and I managed to stagger back to my hotel somehow. In subsequent trips to Tokyo I have attempted to find that bar again but have never succeeded. It is probably better that way.

I have never told Yoshi, my lover now for many years, of my first experience with a Japanese boy. Perhaps I will someday. I will pull him onto my lap and ask him to hold my whisky glass while I drink and feast my eyes on his beautiful face. And then...

THE END

DRESSED FOR AN ERECTION

"Damn it, Mac, I told you this is a high class operation and you can't come to work in those fuckin' shabby levis." The voice was rough and authoritative; it must be the foreman.

"But shit, Rod, I mean sir, there ain't no women around that I've seen, and most of my work clothes are wearin' pretty thin."

That voice was younger but no less masculine. They were obviously workmen constructing the five-story manufacturing facility next door to where I was working at the time.

"Look, Mac, you started out this morning with just a small tear up the seam of your ass, and by now your butt is practically wide open to the world. I been watching you all day, with that hairy crack gettin' more and more exposed and my dick gettin' harder and harder every time you stoop over."

That really made me stop in my tracks, but maybe I should explain where we were and what I was doing there in the first place.

I'm an accountant, and a pretty good one, they tell me. I free-lance, trying to make sense out of other accountants' goofs, so I work for various companies for a few days or a few weeks when they call me to straighten out their messes. This time I was working for a company that was constructing a new building next door as part of their expansion; they assigned me an office on the ground floor next to this construction, and you might guess that the sight of all that brawn and beef in hard hats going back and forth and climbing stairs and ladders right outside my window didn't do much for my concentration.

Have you ever tried to study the details of endless

columns of numbers when the figures that really mattered were outside your window? Muscles stretching and bunching under worn levis, some with holes worn through where hairy skin peeped through, just asking for an avid tongue? Shirts soaked with sweat down the back and under the arms, open to expose hairy chests and brown nipples perched on tight pecs?

The workmen knocked off at four-thirty but I worked until five. All work had stopped and there was no one in sight when I decided to cut across the construction site to where my car was parked. But as I walked along a partially-completed wall I heard these voices on the other side, and that about brings you up to date.

"Come here, Mac, next to these window panes leaning against the wall here. Now look at the reflection of your ass through the tear in those fuckin' levis. Every time you bend over I have a hard time keepin' my mind on business, ya know?"

The end of the wall was just ahead of me, and I cautiously peeked around the corner. I had to see what was going on. There was "Mac", a young workman with a blond mustache and curls to match, orange hard hat in place, bent over with his ass pointed toward the tilted glass. Sure enough, there was a good six-inch tear in his jeans through which his pretty pink asshole was clearly visible. Some light hairs set off the scene, with some darker ones shadowing the center of attraction.

"These levis are so rotten that just a little yank" - burly fists demonstrated the point - "and you're wide open, man." The fists belonged to an older man with gray sprinkles in his full, dark beard and a suggestion of the beginnings of a paunch, also still wearing his hard hat. "Rod" was no chicken, but he was also well built and obviously knew what he wanted. His fingertips traced the now widely gaping tear and the hard muscle beneath.

"Good enough to eat, fucker," he growled, and knelt

behind Mac, his tongue snaking into that enticing crevice. My cock stiffened as I watched. I could almost taste that funky, sweaty asshole, especially when Mac groaned and sighed, pushing back against his foreman's bearded face and gripping his own knees for support.

I figured by this time they wouldn't object too much to having some company so I quietly walked over toward them. Mac's eyes were closed in total enjoyment, but Rod caught a glimpse of me when I came into his line of sight. He didn't bat an eye. He was the foreman, and knew he could do just about anything he wanted in his building. Even when I drew closer, close enough to see the shiny spit coating that blond ass, he just kept lapping and probing, and I knew the young hole was opening up for him.

Eventually he stopped and got to his feet, but Mac didn't change position.

"Jees, Rod, don't stop now! You got my balls riled up and ready - it feels so fuckin' good..."

"This is goin' to feel even better, Mac," the boss growled, unbuttoning his fly. "I been half hard all day, thinkin' of pluggin' your ass that's been peekin' and winkin' at me." He struggled for a minute before extracting a fat, stiff cock that was a good nine-incher and pulling back the loose foreskin over the bulging mushroom head.

"Hey, Rod, I don't know if I can take that - couldn't ya just lick it some more..."

By this time I was standing right next to the foreman and drooling over the sight of that thick prick. Rod grinned at me, knowing that Mac didn't even know I was there and seeing the hunger in my eyes.

He put his thick, calloused finger in his mouth briefly and then pressed it at the pink pucker that was his main interest. "Just a finger to get ya' loosened up a little, Mac." And in it went, slowly but steadily, and Mac groaned louder this time.

"Yeah, that's right, man, open your hot hole up for me," Rod ordered softly, pushing past the second knuckle to the increasing groans he wanted to hear.

I couldn't take much more of this without getting into the act. I knelt by the foreman's side and he immediately shoved that fat dick into my mouth while he fingered his buddy. I tasted the sweat of his crotch and the suggestion of a little cheese accumulated during the day, along with his sweet pre-cum that dripped from the bulbous head. I wanted to tongue it for a while, savoring all those flavors and the masculine aroma from his crotch, but Rod just shoved it into my throat as he finger-fucked his victim.

"Shit, Rod, your finger's as big as most men's dicks, I swear," Mac grunted, but he didn't move away. I could see his knees begin to shake a little with the strain.

Rod pulled his dick part way out of my mouth and then shoved it in deep again, and I managed to get my own cock out, gripping it hard between my knees as the big man face-fucked me in rhythm to the finger-fucking he was giving his friend. But that didn't last long.

"OK, Mac, it's time for the main event," Rod gritted, taking his cock back and beginning to substitute it for his finger. It was my saliva that lubricated it. As the heavy head pressed against the opening, Mac moaned in apprehension.

"Easy, man," he pleaded. "That feels like a huge fuckin' log - "

"Yeah, kid, its goin' in there, like this - up your fuckin' hole, boy," and I watched that pulsing pole, slick with my spit, enter and spread the blond asshole. When it was about half-way in he gripped the young man at both hips and held him steady, letting him get used to it.

Always willing to help, I began to lick the exposed cock shaft and asshole, adding more saliva to ease the situation. The combined taste of cock and asshole was ambrosia, I can tell you.

"What the fuck?" Mac queried, apparently becoming aware of my presence for the first time. He tried to look back over his shoulder, but the foreman's grip wouldn't allow him to turn very far.

"Yeah, I got a helper here, Mac," Rod chuckled. "He's gettin' it nice and slippery, just right to shove it all the way - in!" With one thrust, that huge tool disappeared, and the foreman's black crotch hair pressed against that blond ass, leaving nothing for me to work on.

"Jees, man," Mac grunted and panted. "Fuckin' poker up my asshole! Ugh! Easy, Rod, easy ..."

"Hey, you, whatever your name is, go around to his head and shove your dick in his mouth. Got to keep his mouth full, else he'll just complain." Rod gestured to me with his head.

"Huh?" Mac asked, but I lost no time in following instructions. Mac looked up at my face for just a moment, then down at my stiff prick, and latched onto it with no hesitation. Rod was right; there was no more conversation from Mac. His lips and tongue smacked for a moment around my cockhead and then he took me to the root.

"Maybe next time - you'll think twice - about wearing those - ragged levis - on the job - " Rod muttered as he set up a vicious pace, his thick prick thrusting deep each time and withdrawing most of the way before plowing that blond ass again. Each time he thrust, my own cock went deep into the blond's throat. Mac's hard hat wobbled with the double penetration, but his eyes were closed in total enjoyment, I could tell. "Ummm - ugh - ummm - ugh," was all he could get out.

I watched the expression on the foreman's face and he was watching mine. We both began to show signs of delirium, plugging both holes in the handsome blond.

I watched the foreman's eyes grow rounder and his breathing become more labored.

"Yeah, man - fuckin' you from both ends - hot ass is tight - shovin' all the way in - won't be long - "

"Suck that dick," I added for good measure. "Full of cock in both ends - gettin' my balls boilin' - "

"Yeah, man - goin' to cum in a minute - goin' to shoot up your ass - " Rod snarled, his eyes rolling back in his head.

Mac gobbled happily, pressing back against the onslaught from behind, and with the double sensation of his sucking mouth and the expression on the foreman's face, I couldn't hold back much longer, either.

The foreman groaned and thrust harder than ever before. "Take it, man - cumin' up your ass!" he shouted, his arms wrapped around the blond's hips as he fucked wildly. His eyes were fixed on some point on a ceiling that wasn't even there yet.

Mac took it like a man, hot gism filling his ass. Watching the ecstatic throes of the foreman, his face twisted in a mixture of savagery and joy, I could feel my own explosion building up, especially when Mac clamped down on my dick all the way down his throat.

"Man - ", Rod panted, his thrusts tapering off, "that's a hot ass, just right after a hard day's work." He finally stopped, the sweat dripping from under his hard hat, and studied his cock as he slowly pulled out. Then he looked up and grinned at me, and for some reason that did it - put me over the top. I filled Mac's face with hot juice, taking over where Rod had left off.

"Oh, yeah, take it, man - " I groaned, and noticed that Rod was also watching my facial expressions as I had observed his. Then he tucked his softening cock back in his levis and calmly walked away with a casual wave as I was starting to come down from that exquisite high.

When I pulled out, Mac smacked his lips over what

had dribbled down his chin and stood up for the first time. He looked for Rod but he had disappeared.

"Bastard didn't even get me off after blasting my ass with that fuckin' plank of his," he grumbled.

"Hey, no problem - I'd be only too happy to take care of that," I offered magnanimously.

Without a moment's hesitation he unbuttoned his fly and within seconds I was down on one of the hardest and juiciest cocks I had ever had. It only took a few strokes and he was off, hot juice flooding my tonsils while the aroma of sweaty crotch blanketed my nostrils. My own cock dribbled its last on the bare concrete floor as I took his spicy load.

When he finally finished, I stood up and we started adjusting our clothes.

"Those levis have had it, I would say," I commented, smiling at the gaping rear and wondering how he was going to get home in that condition. "That tear in the seam certainly got your boss heated up."

Mac grinned at me mischievously. "Yeah, it really worked, didn't it? And I got three more pairs at home just like these!"

THE END

93

Relations between employer and
employee can be improved with the
proper dress code, it seems.

RESTSTOP R & R

I was pissed. It was already getting dark, and here we were, in the middle of nowhere in our new mobile home, just because Jerry, my lover, had to go searching for that ultimate camera shot of California scenery.

We were on our way from San Diego to Seattle in our new RV, one of those humongous creations on wheels that seem like they are better than the home you just left but never quite live up to expectations. Jerry is an amateur photographer, so we were taking the back roads in search of dramatic hills and valleys, golden in California summer, shadowed mysteriously by trees and sagebrush and rock formations (or at least that's the way he thinks about those things).

"Hey, there's a rest stop just ahead! See where that truck is turning in?" Jerry grinned at me a little triumphantly, knowing I was disappointed to be so far away from civilization for overnighting.

"Is it the rest stop or the driver of that truck that turns you on?" I grumped, but at least a rest stop was better than nothing.

We turned in and settled like a huge hen near the tractor trailer. There was a pickup camper near the far end of the parking area with a bunch of kids running around it, but otherwise the stop was deserted. The truck driver was alighting from his high cab and making his way toward the brick mensroom.

"See you in a couple of minutes", he grinned at me. Truckers are a favorite prey of his (and mine too, I should admit), so I grinned back at him. I watched his trim, khaki-shorted body move towards the john with my usual satisfaction.

Sure enough, a few minutes later Jerry returned with trucker in tow, introducing him as "Tony". He was no chicken, certainly, but with a dark beard and a bushy mustache over smiling lips and a blue twinkle in his eye. His chest sprouted kinky brown hairs that tumbled out of his shirt in an interesting pattern. I turned on the small light over the sink to replace the setting sun.

"This is Cal, my lover," Jerry explained. Tony looked me up and down, obviously wondering if this was going to be a threeway. Apparently he approved as indicated by a spreading smile and an obvious grope of his crotch.

He was a pretty sexy guy, broad shouldered and husky, greasy levis and all. His crotch bulge was growing under my interested gaze.

Jerry led the way toward the bedroom at the end of the mobile home. "Let's get you out of those sweaty clothes." I tagged along, not yet sure how I felt about the whole thing.

Tony sat on the bed and Jerry started to remove his greasy engineer boots. Soon he had the moist, raunchy feet in his grasp, and started to lick them clean, glorying in their ripe aroma. I watched with increasing interest, my own cock swelling strongly in the leather shorts I had worn all day.

"Yeah, suck 'em dry and clean," Tony breathed, a wide grin splitting his swarthy face. He leaned on his elbows, watching Jerry service him avidly.

I unfastened the trucker's belt and eased open his fly. Tony helped by groping my hardon through my leather shorts. He seemed to know what he wanted, and it wasn't necessarily clean feet!

Jerry started to tug down the greasy levis, and my eyes popped open when a fat ten incher reared its beautiful head as the pants were removed. Jerry gave that little growl I knew so well when he saw something he really liked. I couldn't say I blamed him.

"Beautiful prick," he breathed, and Tony grinned.

"Ain't had any for a couple of days, so it ought to be

a pretty good meal - for somebody," Tony said, glancing at me. Jerry didn't notice, his fist encircling the thick shaft and milking it slowly. Tony helped out by unbuttoning his shirt, revealing a broad, hairy chest with pert nipples on firm pecs.

Jerry leaned forward and took the swollen cockhead into his mouth, catching the pearly drop of pre-cum that had developed there. He moaned in immediate enjoyment, as did Tony. The trucker leaned back, reveling in the hot contact, especially when Jerry began to move his tongue around the ridge and work his way down. My own dick was beginning to jerk with the visual stimulation; sometimes I really like to watch - for a while.

At that moment there was a quiet but decisive knock at the side door of the RV. Neither Jerry nor Tony appeared to notice. Probably some tourist wanting information, I thought. I noticed that it was entirely dark by this time, the only light being the small one in the kitchen in the center of the vehicle where the door was.

I opened the door and started slightly at the sight of the Highway Patrol officer standing there, a tall stud with a blond mustache framing his smile.

"Sorry to disturb you, sir," the officer smiled up at me politely under the motorcycle helmet. "I'm late on my rounds - had trouble with the bike, so arrived after the men's room was closed for the night. I saw your light and wondered if I could use yours?"

I was too flustered to react except to stammer, "Why sure, officer," and stepped back to allow him to enter. As he came in, the imposing figure was even more exciting, with the broad shoulders that carried the leather jacket to perfection, the tan trousers hugging his trim buns and muscular thighs, to say nothing about the gun and holster clinging to his hip. His glossy boots had a patina of road dust on them.

He looked me up and down, also. All I wore was

those leather shorts, and his eyes flicked from my bare chest to my crotch where the hardon was still showing prominently. His lips curved just a fraction, tilting his dark blond mustache up a millimeter or two, and then he was all official courtesy again.

"Uh - this way?" he asked, since I had made no attempt to point out the john. I nodded, but then I realized the problem; the john was off the hall just outside the bedroom door where Jerry and the trucker were balling, and the door was wide open! What do I do now?

But he had caught the nod and was heading that way. As he approached I could see that his eye was caught by whatever was going on in there, and I hurried after him, not sure what I could do about the inevitable confrontation.

As I caught up with him I could see Jerry and Tony stretched on the bed in a cozy and engulfing sixty-nine, totally oblivious of the scrutiny being paid to them. I don't think they had even missed me, and they certainly didn't know we had a visitor! Anybody with half an eye could see what was going on, and the CHP had two beautiful ones, with twenty-twenty vision, no doubt.

The officer turned to me with a grin on his face and whispered, "Friends of yours?"

I decided to try to make the best of it. "One of them is - the other is a trucker."

"Figures," he chuckled and went into the dark bathroom. Well, what the hell, I thought? It's our "house", isn't it?

Thinking quickly, I slid the pocket door shut silently, shutting out the amorous couple from further scrutiny, and followed him into the bathroom.

"The switch is over here, by the sink," I offered, switching it on and leaning back against the wall. The officer looked gratefully at me and started to open his fly.

"Been traveling far?" he asked casually as he extracted his cock. My gaze fixed on his meaty tool, even though I tried not to look. He seemed so casual and I was flustered as hell.

"Uh - not too far," I stammered, feeling my hardon starting to take on new life. His cock arched out from those tan twills like a fleshy beacon, the head partially covered with a succulent foreskin.

His stream started strong but quickly tapered off as if a clamp had suddenly tightened. He looked down at it, concentrating on restarting the stream, but nothing happened. I knew exactly how he felt, I couldn't have pissed either. I decided to take the initiative.

"Having a problem?" I asked softly.

He looked up at me quickly, a slight blush tingeing his cheeks. "Guess so," he admitted a little sheepishly.

"Maybe I can help," I offered magnanimously, throwing all caution to the winds. I reached out and grasped it gently, as if to help him out of his predicament.

After the first slight withdrawal, he seemed to relax but his cock sure didn't. It grew steadily under my tender care, lengthening and thickening gloriously.

"Seems my little problem is getting bigger," he opined, still with a little twinkle in his eye.

"Sure, is," I agreed, "and beautifully, too." It was growing thick and stiff under my helpful care, rearing high and throbbing. Our eyes met for a probing instant; we both knew what was going to happen, and it wasn't your typical tourist-CHP exchange!

I knelt on the floor, the rough leather of my shorts scraping my stiff dick deliciously as I knelt to do homage to another obviously "in need". He turned slightly toward me as my tongue caressed the flaring head.

I didn't wait for the usual amenities but proceeded all the way down in a slow, steady progression, and I could feel his legs tense with the moist heat. His prick filled my mouth and lodged deep in my throat, and I moaned around it as I tasted his sweet meat. He thrust forward involuntarily, impaling me even more.

I grasped his hips, encountering his thick belt and the gun in his holster. It added a special touch of implied violence that made my head swim. How many times had I fantasized about a moment like this when seeing handsome CHPs roaring down the highway on their shiny bikes, sirens wailing and lights flashing?

I pulled him tightly against my face, the cock rigidly filling my throat, and began to ride it up and down in great slurps. I glanced up at his face. His eyes were closed in total involvement, it seemed, and he rocked a little on his heels, the shiny black boots squeaking softly. But soon he reached down and pulled me to my feet and immediately gripped my stiff dick through my shorts.

"Looks like you've got a similar problem," he smiled, his cock twitching damply in the yellowish light of the bathroom.

"It's no problem," I smiled back, my grin growing wider as he put one arm around me to fondle my ass through the leather shorts while his grip tightened on my throbbing dick.

"Into the living room," he ordered gruffly, an order I was happy to obey. I led him to the darkened room at the other end of the RV and he immediately pulled me against him from the rear, his cock thrusting against my ass. Then I felt his fingers at the waistband, unsnapping and opening them broadly. He lowered my shorts and pushed me down so I supported my torso with my arms braced against the couch, my feet still on the floor.

He grasped my naked buns in his broad hands with an appreciative grunt. "Pretty nice, guy," he murmured, and before I knew what was happening, I felt his lips kissing my ass and his tongue lapping its way toward my center. His boots creaked again as he knelt behind me.

"Open that ass, boy," he ordered, and I shuddered at the command and at the prospect of taking that huge poker. But first his tongue probed and lapped my asshole, his bristly mustache grinding the sensitive crack. His helmet grazed my back as he pressed deeper.

He came up for air once or twice. "Real man's ass," he grunted. His tongue dove deeper and deeper, and I was wild for that forbidding prick.

"Goin' to fuck your ass." A simple statement of fact, and I knew it was true. I could feel him spreading saliva on the head and shaft, but wondered if that would be enough.

"Relax, baby, I'm comin' in!" And sure enough, that hot, tasty mushroom pressed against me and quickly pushed into me, immediately filling my ass with steamy CHP prick. I moaned but there was no let-up; he continued shoving all that tool into me in a slow, steady movement until I felt the tan twills pressing against my ass.

He only let it soak for a few moments before beginning a rhythmic thrust-and-withdraw cycle that weakened my knees. "Yeah, hot ass, fucker," he groaned, gripping my hips as he thrust, allowing no deviation from his single-minded purpose. "You love hot prick up your ass, don't ya?"

"Yes, sir," I moaned, pushing back against the huge prong spreading me wide. He gripped my cock in one hand and my balls in the other. I sagged willingly into his masterful clutches.

"Got a load built up for a guy like you," he gritted, picking up his speed, lurching heavily into me and reaching internal spots never reached before. His iron grip on my cock and balls was hurting deliciously. I was just a willing receptacle for his aggression, and I loved it.

"Goin' ta fill your ass full, man," he gasped, his cock

swelling even more, his thrusts even deeper and harder. I couldn't wait for the final onslaught, and it was not long in coming. Heavy thrusts in rapid succession, his breath hot on my neck, his arms wrapped around me possessively, my cock and balls throbbing under the welcome torture.

"Right - about - now!" he groaned. He thrust hard, and I could feel the jerking of his spending prick, filling me full of hot CHP cream. Over and over he plunged, unloading bolt after bolt of steamy cum, while I quivered weakly in his consuming grasp. Finally he slowed and stopped, his breath coming in ragged gasps. His grip on my screaming cock and balls relaxed.

"Good, man," he sighed, straightening slowly, his cock still deeply embedded. I couldn't answer, not with all that meat up my ass. And then he slowly withdrew, his cock slipping free almost reluctantly, it seemed, and I was suddenly very empty.

Slowly I turned around to face him. He had worn his helmet all that time, and his face was in shadow with the light behind him, but I could see a satisfied gleam in his eye and a slight smile curving his lips as he stuffed his spent cock back into his uniform.

He grinned as he readjusted his clothes and hitched his gun belt back in place. "Never know what's going to happen in one of these rest stops." He glanced at my cock, jerking stiffly, but turned toward the door.

"Got to be getting home. Wife's probably wondering where I am by now."

As he stepped down from the RV, I noticed his big, white Kawasaki leaning on its kickstand, waiting patiently for its master to return. He saluted smartly and swung aboard, the engine quietly coming alive at his touch of the starter. And then he was gone.

Still shaking I returned to the bedroom, quietly sliding open the pocket door. Jerry and the trucker were still sixty-nining, sprawled diagonally across the bed, but this time the trucker was on top, his ass and Jerry's head near the edge of the bed. Jerry looked up at me from the trucker's crotch with a glazed expression, his mouth full of cock pumping deeply into his throat. He was obviously in heaven, but my own cock was about to turn blue from pent up pressure.

I caressed the hairy ass inches away from Jerry's face as he watched me, knowing what I had in mind. The trucker didn't seem to object, concentrating on sucking Jerry's cock down his throat.

I smeared some lubricant - we could use lubricant this time! - on my cock from the supply next to the bed. Just the touch of my hand and the cool grease started my cock jerking, and the ecstatic moans of the other guys added to my own excitement. I smeared some on his hairy ass and inserted my fingertip, but he was obviously ready. Without further delay I pushed my cock into the trucker a little way and he merely wriggled. Like it or not, I was going in!

I pushed hard and buried my boner to the balls in one steady move. The trucker moaned but merely pushed deeper into Jerry's throat. Jerry was watching me excitedly, the trucker's and my balls almost in his face. He helped by spreading the hairy cheeks with his hands that were already clasping the trucker's hips to his face.

It was hot and clenched me hard, bringing my temperature close to the boiling point almost immediately. I might not be a CHP stud, but that trucker would know he'd been fucked when I finished with him. I set up a rapid fire action. I needed that asshole, and he was going to get it!

With each thrust I shoved the trucker's cock deep into Jerry's gobbling craw. I couldn't see him anymore, but I knew Jerry was grooving on the scene, watching me fuck the guy at close range while sucking that monster cock at the same time.

Both guys started to groan, and it seemed like things were quickly drawing to a head. I knew I couldn't hold off long, not after that hot scene with the CHP.

"All right, you guys, suck those dicks 'cause I'm goin' to fill this trucker's ass - hot fuckin' asshole - suck'em up, boys, goin' to cum - right - now!" I groaned and shoved hard, simultaneous with a chorus of groans and slurps from Jerry and Tony who were apparently cuming in great gobs at the same time.

"Yeah, take it, man!" I shouted, and Tony took it, his body wobbling wildly under the double onslaught. My prick jerked and shot stream after stream of liquid lava into that hot ass, sending me over the brink of sanity for several minutes, it seemed.

Jerry was the last to quiet, continuing to thrust up into Tony's mouth even after he was drained. When all was quiet I slowly pulled out and looked down at Jerry, his mouth still full of trucker tool. His eyes were shining with joy and, yes, love, for me.

As my cock slipped free, I squeezed out one last drop of cum that landed on Jerry's forehead. I could see him try to grin, which only really took shape when Tony rolled to the side and Jerry's mouth was emptied. I bent down and kissed him on the lips, tasting the sweet-salty cum that Tony had deposited.

We all had a beer while catching our breaths, and then Tony went to sleep in his cab. Jerry looked at me a little quizzically.

"What happened to you while we were getting warmed up?"

"Oh, nothing much," I answered, starting to get dinner ready. "What could happen in a rest stop?"

THE END

GO FOR BROKER

As a real estate broker I meet all kinds of people, many of them real duds, but when Mr. T. D. Selby walked in my office I quickly decided he was something else. From his fresh but mature face framed by dark wavy hair with a tinge of grey at the temples, to his broad shoulders set off by a dark, fashionable suit, to the bulging crotch and muscular legs under the pin-striped material, the impression was just short of spectacular. He was obviously a man who knew what he wanted and would claim it when he found it.

I quickly arranged a chair for him and sat opposite while I listened to his requirements for a business building in my neighborhood. I could barely keep my gaze away from the thick basket that stretched the crotch of his pants as he sat with knees spread and looked directly into my eyes as we talked. I guess I wasn't too obvious, since he maintained his cool, business-like attitude throughout.

"I only have one building that might be right for you at the moment, but it is still under construction," I said when he had finished listing his requirements.

"I don't mind a construction mess," he replied. "Let's see it." So he followed me (in my thrifty Chevrolet) in his Mercedes to the site I had in mind, a two-story renovated building on the edge of a redevelopment area downtown. The trip gave me a chance to calm down and remind myself that this was strictly business.

I had a key so we entered unannounced. The main floor at the street level was empty, with no workmen around at the time. Since it was nearly lunch time, the workers may have been on their break, but the space appeared finished, as much as it would be until a new owner or renter had been contracted. Mr. Selby looked around carefully. Again I could tell he knew his way around and quickly grasped the possibilities of the place.

"I'm afraid it may be too small," he said thoughtfully, but continued his survey.

"The basement floor is still under construction," I said. "We can see that also if you wish."

"Go ahead - I'll be down after I have had another look around." So I proceeded down the back stairs into a dark cavern of ghostly studs (vertical rows of two by fours, I mean) outlining the office spaces to be built there. The lights had not been installed, but there was an illuminated area at the far end, apparently from extension cord flood lights for the present work. I groped my way toward the light, and then began to hear voices.

"Aren't you going to eat that second sandwich, Steve?" a husky voice inquired from the shadows.

"You got my favorite lunch between your legs, Mac," was the reply.

"Yeah, but - hey, what are you - do you think its safe here - oh, Christ, you got a hot mouth - ummm, yeah, man, that feels so fuckin' good - "

As you can imagine, my ears pricked up (more than just an expression) and I made sure my cautious advance toward that circle of light was quiet. I didn't want to interrupt anything.

Finally I could see the two workmen at the edge of the lighted area, in hardhats and with tools strapped to their waists. Their levis were worn and faded and you could understand how they got that way; one of the guys was on his knees on the concrete floor, servicing a thick, towering cock thrusting upward through the fly of the other workman seated on a pile of unused lumber. I remained in the darkness, my eyes glued to the scene.

"Yeah, take it all the way into your throat," Mac groaned, leaning backward to enjoy that hot mouth. That was a tall order but apparently Steve was succeeding pretty well. Alternating a tongue bath around the bulging

106

head with dives down that massive column, he buried his nose in the dark pubic hair protruding from the gaping fly.

"Yeah, pull on my balls while you do that," Mac gritted, his head thrown back and eyes closed in rapture. Steve obediently fished out two hairy balls and twisted and pulled them not too gently as he continued his mission.

My own cock was approaching the same state as Mac's, and I fished it out (with some difficulty), all thoughts of anything but that magnificent coupling in the dimness erased from my brain. Any guilt I may have felt about watching a private scene was wiped out by the heat I was beginning to feel in my balls.

"Hey, better stop, Steve," Mac grunted struggling upward. "I'm set to pop, and I need some of that big blond meat before its too late!"

Steve rose to his feet with a grin. "Thought it was gettin' real juicy, Mac - I almost had ya that time," he said as he quickly opened his pants and they slid half-down his husky thighs. Out popped a thick staff of pink prick with a darker head peeking out of a stretched foreskin. The two boners were about equal in size, more than filling the grip of the calloused fists around them. The main difference was the dark bush in Mac's crotch and the blond one setting off Steve's throbbing joystick.

Mac shoved Steve's hand aside and pulled him close, his hand pulling the foreskin over the head before running his tongue around under it. Steve stiffened and quivered as his buddy brought him to the threshold of excitement, and I could almost taste the warm muskiness of that cockhead myself. Not having a foreskin myself, I appreciated that added touch and approved Mac's nibbling as he proceeded to chow down on that tender meat.

"Shit, man, you know how to do it," Steve rumbled, his knees buckling slightly under the pressure. "Nibble that foreskin - fuckin' hot mouth," he moaned. "Yeah, take it!" He thrust forward, shoving his pulsing pole deep into Mac's throat as the cocksucker allowed the foreskin to retract. "Uh, yeah -" Mac held him tight to his face with one hand on each curving bun.

The scratching by my zipper irritated me, so I opened the waistband of my slacks to ease the problem. My hand was flailing my overheated prick while I watched Mac beat his own and gobble that rigid rod.

Suddenly I realized I was not alone in my dark niche, but there was no time to react; strong arms encircled my waist and my stiff cock was gripped from behind in a steely fist. I jerked in surprise.

"Interesting construction," Mr. Selby muttered in my ear, pressing hard against me from the rear and watching the workmen over my shoulder. I don't know how long he had been behind me, but I could feel his stiffness against my ass. He set up his own rhythm on my dick, my sticky pre-cum lubricating his hand. What a way to handle a client! I thought fleetingly, although at this point it was the client who was handling me! But then there was a new development in the lighted circle.

"Bend down over this heap of lumber," Mac ordered suddenly, and as Steve assumed the position, his ripe buns bathed in yellow light, Mac knelt and began to rim his buddy's hot ass. "Oh, yeah," Steve sighed, giving his ass a little wiggle and seating Mac's face even deeper in the cleft. "Ummmm," Mac mumbled, and my own cock gave an extra lurch in Mr. Selby's firm grip.

Without breaking his rhythm, Mr. Selby eased my pants down and I felt his fingers caressing my hole. The touch was so gentle and teasing that it could have been Mac's tongue just as well. And then suddenly it *was* a tongue, Mr. Selby crouching behind me and spreading my cheeks for that darting warmth that opened me up as nothing else could do. With his hand continuing to stroke my throbbing cock and his tongue probing my asshole to the depths, I was soon a trembling wreck threatening to explode.

"Fuck me, Mac - go ahead and ram it in," Steve begged, his voice strained and muffled against the stacked lumber. "Let me have that big prick all the way - "

Mac wasted no time in following his instructions. He rose and immediately positioned that fat rammer at the wet hole he had just prepared. He pressed slowly inward as Steve groaned and moaned, clawing at the boards under him. "Big, fuckin' prick," Steve gasped. "Hot, fuckin' asshole," Mac responded breathlessly, pushing in relentlessly.

I guess Mr. Selby decided I was relaxed enough at that point, because he rose and I felt his broad, spongy-firm cockhead at my opening. With his free arm he pulled me back against him, and an incredibly large prong began its irresistible entry into my defenseless asshole. I hadn't ever seen the thick meat that had strained the crotch of his pants, but I soon felt the enormity as it spread me open. There was no escape even if I had wanted to; as I had surmised, Mr. Selby was a man who took what he wanted when he wanted it.

I tried to stifle my gasps since I didn't want to reveal our presence to the workmen. I guess I shouldn't have worried, because those two guys were oblivious of us and everything else, it seemed. By the time Mr. Selby hit bottom and I felt his hairy balls pressed against me, Mac had struck up a punishing rhythm, thrusting deep and withdrawing almost all the way, the giant prick plundering his buddy in the most enjoyable way I can think of.

"Oh, Christ, yeah - " Steve groaned, and I could almost feel his own stiff stabber grating against the rough lumber with each plunge. Meanwhile I was trying to get used to ten inches of thick prick in my gut without shooting my wad all over the place.

"Think you can handle my business?" Mr. Selby whispered in my ear.

"Just try me - sir!" I groaned, remembering to be polite, and the next thing I knew that "business" was set in motion, in and out, deep and shallow, massive fullness and yawning emptiness alternating to boil my juices toward the surface. The head of his dick must have been even larger than I thought, because each time he pulled back it gave my prostate a twinge that I could feel in my own cockhead. His breath rasped in my ear as we bent forward, and he was muttering, "Hot, sweet butt - tight man asshole - ", things like that.

Mac was really putting it to Steve. His hardhat jarred and jiggled as he fucked the blond ass. The copious black hair on his thighs contrasted sharply with the soft, blond fuzz of his buddy's ass, and his balls slapped his buddy's blond ones with each plunge.

"Goin' to fill your pretty ass," he moaned suddenly, his voice rising. "Goin' to cum up your chute, man!"

"Yeah, do it, Mac - gimme your fuckin' juice!" Steve almost yelled, his ass shoving back toward his buddy yearningly.

One more thrust and he was there, lodged deep in that craven cavern, and I could see him tremble and writhe as he shot his wad deep in that velvet void. Mr. Selby gasped as he watched and plundered his own willing victim, and his hand froze on my dick, gripping hard. His pace quickened until I was a quivering mass of jelly, that huge hammer my only firm support.

Mac began to thrust in and out again but weaker now, his virility temporarily depleted, and then he pulled out with a plop.

"Turn over, Steve, I want to take you right now!" Mac ordered.

Steve rolled over, his cock jabbing for the sky, almost ready to explode. So was I. And when Mac dove down on that rigid ramrod I couldn't hold back any longer. I gushed all over Mr. Selby's hand just as Steve boiled hot in Mac's mouth, frothy cum spurting from two cocks at once. And then there were three - Mr. Selby groaned and shot deep in my gut, too, that stiff stabber jerking and jabbing in my battered bunghole.

It seemed to go on forever, that three-way cum, and with each twitch of Mr. Selby's cock in my ass I gave him another spurt in his hand. Steve thrust upward again and again while Mac tried to swallow it all. Mac's cock was still dribbling a little on the concrete as it slowly softened.

For a moment the four of us locked in a frozen tableau. Our climaxes were over but we were not quite ready to take up where we had left off. Mac still held Steve's cock deep in his throat while Steve regained his breath. Mr. Selby remained deeply imbedded in my ass and still held me tightly as his labored breathing gradually calmed. And I was perfectly content to stay there in his arms, his hand gripping my softening cock, as long as he wished.

Then the two workmen were grinning at each other, Steve leaning on his elbows and Mac crouched between his legs. "Guess we better get back to work," Steve suggested reluctantly. "Yeah, I suppose so. No telling when that real estate broker might show up, and we want to have as much done as possible."

As they pulled up their pants and settled their tool-ladened belts, Mr. Selby slipped out and stepped back. I retrieved my pants and wiped my cock with my hankerchief, wondering how I should react now. I silently followed my client up the back stairs and to the first floor. He turned to me, his hand calmly outstretched in a business-like manner. Except for a slight grin at the corners of his mouth, he seemed exactly as poised and meticulous as when he had walked into my office.

111

"As I thought, this place is not quite what I need. But let me know if something comes up -" his eyes flickered to my crotch - "or you have any other openings that might interest me."

THE END

SHOOTING STARS

The door opened unexpectedly, pulling me back from my reverie.

"Morning, Sam. What's new?"

The deep, resonant voice from one of the handsomest men on earth stirred me as it continued to stir thousands of gay men throughout the country. When Kevin Kolman - a stage name, I didn't know his real one - said, "Suck my cock", thousands of men from all walks of life fell to their knees, salivating. At least that's the way it appeared from sales figures of every porno video he had made, and I had the figures to prove it.

"Not much, stud. Just going over some old photos and promos from days gone by. This is our twentieth year in the skin flick business, you know, and I'm thinking of celebrating. Haven't worked out the details yet. What are you doing here on such a gorgeous day when there is no shooting?"

"I left my harness here the other day and thought I had better get it before someone borrows it for a hot date," he answered absentmindedly, looking over my shoulder at the dozens of glossies spread out on the desk in front of me. "Who are all these guys?"

"Porn stars from years gone by. Even twenty years ago there were favorites who attained some notoriety in the underground." I tried to concentrate on the conversation instead of the packed crotch that was close and at eye level as he leaned over my desk. I knew that beauty intimately from directing and producing him in dozens of situations with other guys, my video cameras seeing all, close and far, the lights poised just right to bring out every vein, every skin fold in that prick of pricks.

Kevin was fiddling with my name sign. "What kind of a name is 'Nosajck', anyway? I always wondered."

113

"Armenian, originally. That was many generations ago. I wonder what my ancestors would have thought about my making porno films? Of course twenty years ago it was sixteen millimeter film and all black and white at first, but there has always been a market for men balling men. I got started in this business that way myself, twenty years ago."

"Yeah?" Kevin seemed incredulous. Then he hastened to try to correct the impression. "Not that it's so unbeliev-able - you still have a good body, from what I can see, but that full beard and the loose, casual clothes you always wear - somehow it doesn't conjure up - " He stammered to a stop. "I mean you always seemed the type to have a family at home, good solid citizen, that sort of thing - "

I was a little miffed, I must admit. Sure, I'd been married once but that only lasted six months when I found out that guys were my speed. I didn't like to think about those days, leaving my bride of six months like that, especially for a real loser, as he turned out. Not that I had a choice, about being gay, I mean. And I still had a damn good sex life, off camera of course. Just because I was no longer a matinee idol -

"Hey, who's this guy?" he asked, putting a finger on one black and white picture.

I stared for a moment at the man he had indicated. Why did he have to pick out that one of all the possible pictures in the stack?

"Guy named Jason Samuels - at least that was his stage name. He had a pretty good run for quite a while," I answered shortly.

"He's gorgeous," Kevin breathed. "Have you got any of his old films?"

"Sure, I have originals or first copies of all our films, gathering dust in the back room." I hoped he wouldn't make the rather obvious connections in our names.

114

"Could I see one of them?" Kevin persisted.

I exhaled slowly, hesitating. "Yeah - I'd have to set up the old projector, and it would be black and white, but - sure, I guess so."

"Would you mind, Sam?" Kevin almost breathed in my ear. I couldn't resist that masculine charm any more than his millions of fans. That resonant voice from that gorgeous face, the flashing blue eyes under the perfect dark brows, and the masculine but sensitive face could produce a boner on just about any gay guy, even ignoring the perfect, trim musculature revealed when he stripped down. And that cock!

We went back to the archives and chatted while I checked the old inventory sheets for the right bin.

"You got a lover, Kevin?" I inquired casually.

"No, Sam, I live with my mother. She never remarried after my father left, and she gets pretty lonely - " he broke off awkwardly and I didn't press the issue. "But I make out OK, even without a place of my own." I was pretty sure of that.

After a lengthy search of the index and through the dusty film cans I found one of Jason Samuels I thought he might like. Kevin sat in a tired old molded chair, seemingly unaware of how sexy he was with his legs spread and his bulging basket stretching his levis. I threaded the film into the projector and switched off the lights, and soon the flickering figure of Jason Samuels, in the act of undressing, filled the screen. He was about six feet tall but with unusually broad shoulders and deepset eyes under rather heavy dark brows.

"Good looking guy."

Kevin watched in silence until Jason slowly let his pants fall and straining jockey shorts were revealed. It was customary in those days for the actor to play with it in his shorts for awhile, but within a couple of minutes the lengthening bulge protruded from the top of the waistband, and Kevin groaned in admiration.

At that point in the story, another actor entered, supposedly catching Jason unaware, and after a couple of sentences (there was no sound, of course), he proceeded to pull down the jockeys, letting it all hang out.

We both reacted to that shot but in different ways. I suddenly was struck by the similarities between "Jason's" and Kevin's equipment - about the same size and appearance, even to the slight upward curve in the shaft that made sixty-nining particularly good. Kevin groaned again and clutched his crotch that seemed to be under some turmoil. "Beautiful!" he breathed. "And a beautiful man!" he added, almost to himself.

I tried not to let Kevin see how this filming was upsetting me. His obvious turn-on was only one element of the confusion in my brain at that moment. We watched as the other actor - I had forgotten his name after all those years - then proceeded to strip, giving Jason's rigid cock a caress or two from time to time. Kevin's breaths grew shorter as he watched. I tried to ignore him, but that was impossible.

Then the second man knelt, his own dick brushing the floor, and started working on Jason's prong. First the head, and then licking down the shaft and fondling his pendulous balls.

"Beautiful!" Kevin breathed. I turned to look at him and he had actually taken out his own rod, that famous tool that everyone drooled over.

I was no exception. I had never before been in a situation like this with Kevin, just the two of us with no cameras running. To be that close to such a masculine idol with his cock in his fist, even with my jaded background, was tough. I tried to concentrate on the film, but my eyes kept straying to Kevin stroking his dripping dong.

Finally the actor tried to take all that prick in his mouth. He was good, but not that good. Fully three inches remained untouched, even as he strained to force it all the way down his throat. Kevin almost sobbed with excitement.

"Damn it, Kevin, if you don't put that thing away I may break a rule and suck off one of my actors myself," I growled, more intrigued than I liked to admit.

Kevin looked at me blankly for a moment. "I wouldn't mind if you did, Sam," he said quietly. "That guy Jason really turns me on."

I stared at the screen for a moment, my pulse racing. Jason and the actor were by now in a sixty-nine position, but the camera concentrated on Jason's cock being slurped by the unknown actor. My mind was suddenly made up. I moved down to kneel between Kevin's spread knees and began to do homage to that prick that had launched unknown thousands of bolts of cum world-wide.

It was as good as it looked. I've sucked a lot of cocks in the last twenty years - the number must be close to five figures - but I couldn't take it all, either.

"Yeah, suck it," Kevin crooned, but I couldn't tell if he was talking to me or to the actors on screen. Maybe both. I fished out his heavy balls, always kept shaven for the camera, and rolled them between my fingers as I forced more and more of that tremendous tool down my avid gullet. He didn't actually have a foreskin, not that was long enough to cover the head, but enough to slide down to the crown and a little bit more - truly a luxurious lob of at least ten inches.

I finally managed to get most of it in, until his pubic hair tickled my nose and I could get a whiff of his exquisite crotch. No sissy perfumes there, just a little healthy sweat. Again I envied all the other studs, guys of all descriptions, who had been privileged to swing on this man in all the videos I had made of him.

I needed a breather and his nuts drew me. Stroking his wet cock slowly with one hand, I shifted to tongue those orbs and suck them into my mouth, one at a time. There was no way to get both of them in, they were just too big. Kevin groaned with this action - at least I think my ministrations were responsible for his agonized sound. He raised up and slipped his pants down to his ankles, giving me full range to worship as was his due. His hairy thighs spread widely but his eyes were still fixed on the screen.

"That guy can't take it all. Hell, nobody could take all of that! I wish it was in color - "

My view was in color, and to emphasize it I rolled his shirt up so I could play with his nipples, perched on the peaks of hairy, rounded pecs. I sighted up over that fabulous tanned washboard belly where probably hundreds of loads had been deposited, on screen and off. His prick throbbed straight and tall over me like a skyscraper in an otherwise elegant but subdued landscape.

His nipples tensed and pouted under my fingers, and I tweaked and twisted them none too gently. I knew he wasn't too turned on by tit play so I didn't persist, but they were there when I wanted them.

I returned to his crotch and the moist balls. My fingertips roamed backward from his sack and he immediately took the cue, at least partly aware of my lustful intentions. He shoved down to the edge of the chair, and I immediately moved back, back toward that hairless asshole that nobody had ever entered, to my knowledge. He had it is his contract that he was not to be fucked, but there was no prohibition against rimming!

I lapped his hole gently at first, and he hummed with enjoyment. It was tightly closed, but tasted like ambrosia. Around the hole, then in the hole, and he was squirming lower in his chair, his breaths coming faster and harder. In that position I couldn't do a very good handjob, and so he took over. He grabbed it in a hairy fist and slowly milked it up and down while I lapped and probed, going gradually deeper as his hole relaxed. Looking up, his balls rested hotly on my nose, and eventually he brought both hands to bear on that stiff shaft stabbing skyward. There was plenty of room for both hands.

I worked my way back to his prick after giving his balls another tonguing. Again I gobbled as much in as I could, leaving plenty of saliva for good lubrication, and then traveled downward again to his balls and asshole. This time I added my finger to my tongue, caressing around the tight muscle ring. He spread his knees widely, giving me full access to his most intimate parts, and I took full advantage of it.

"Shit, he's goin' to fuck that guy!" Kevin moaned. Momentarily I looked up at the flickering screen while leaving my finger in place between his legs. The actor was on all fours and Jason was massaging his own prick, postponing the inevitable plunge into the guy's beckoning ass as he had been instructed to do by the director. That delay always brought out the squirms in the audience, looking forward to that decisive plunge. He was actually spreading lubricant on it, but the audience wasn't aware of that.

Kevin was still, seemingly transfixed by the tension of the moment on screen. I took the opportunity to tackle his rearing rod again while allowing my roaming finger to tickle his asshole. As I sucked down to the root, I could feel his hole twitching, and slowly, gently, I entered him. There was no resistance, so as I picked up my rhythm on his dick, my finger slowly probed deeper and deeper into his ass, the hot, clenching tunnel bidding me on.

"Ugh!" he grunted once, and I stopped for a moment, his prick deep in my throat. I may have dreamed it, but I thought I felt him move down and toward me a fraction.

"That beautiful prick is in to the root!" he gasped, and my finger followed suit, pressing in to the full length until I could feel his young prostate pulsing under my touch.

119

I began to suck furiously then, and to move my finger tip from side to side, caressing that budding gland that was already tensing ominously. Up and down that tremendous shaft I sucked, glorying to the sweet precum that oozed over my tongue and the burgeoning blossoming of his lovebud deep inside.

"He fucks like a horse!" Kevin gasped, and I picked up my pace, doing a little in-and-outing as well as back-and-forthing with my finger. His entire frame was rigid, living through the fuck scene on screen with the sensations I was producing in reality, and that couldn't go on for too long, I knew.

"He's cuming, he's cuming!" Kevin yelled - and so was Kevin. One last shove of my finger up his ass, one last dive down his cock shaft, and I was flooded with rich cream in torrents that usually covered the belly of his partner. Thick spurts, again and again, that would have reached his partner's chin if I hadn't gobbled every drop down. That was something his partners in skin flicks couldn't do, and I knew that was their frequent regret. I didn't blame them; it was straight from the gods.

I didn't have to check the screen to know that Kevin was precisely in tune with Jason. As Jason's spurts tapered off, Kevin began to relax and I managed to swallow his precious load. And then he went limp as my finger withdrew, sagging heavily in the molded chair with a happy smile on his face. It was not until then that I realized that I had cum in my pants sometime along the way.

The film had run through and the loose end was flapping in the abrupt silence in the room. Kevin grinned at me as I rose to turn off the projector. I switched on the lights and busied myself rewinding the film, suddenly concerned that what had happened might make a difference in our future relationship. I could hear him pulling his pants up, and then he came up behind me, put his arms around my waist, and actually purred into my ear.

"Hey, Sam, that was tremendous. I'm really glad it happened - and glad I was able to see that film. That Jason Samuels was really something! Hope I can be that good some day."

I turned around, searching his eyes, but there was no deceit there - he was as sincere as I had ever seen him.

"Hey, you are, stud. You're one of the greatest. Jason Samuels was a bum compared to you."

Kevin's smile grew wider. "Don't shit me, Sam - we are all pretenders these days. But it's nice of you to say that. I have sort of come to think of you as a buddy - no, more a father, I guess. And I really love you for it." He kissed me on the lips, something I had never seen him do with his tricks.

"Funny," he said as he started to leave, "my mother said my father's name was Sam, too. He never knew that he had a son - she never told him. Well, take it easy - and thanks."

THE END

The younger generation can learn
from the older, but sometimes its
more vice than versa.

BOOT-SLAVE TRAINING

There was bare skin everywhere; tanned skin, pale skin, hairy and hairless, clear pink and pimply, but unmistakably male. That was what was so exciting.

It was my first time in such close proximity to all that male flesh. Brought up in the country with few boys my own age, I suddenly realized what I had missed, and was confused by the involuntary quivering in my legs and darting of my eyes away from my assigned tasks toward that magnetic skin tautened by maturing muscles as the other guys, apparently entirely comfortable in their white shorts and nearly-nude camaraderie, fumbled with their mattresses and fart-sacks and argued over whether they were assigned to top or bottom bunks.

"'Ten-shun!" The door to the old wooden barracks had burst open and the imposing figure of "The Chief" seemed to glower down at us mere earthlings. His spotless uniform with dizzying rows of gold stripes running down his left sleeve, his gleaming shoes planted solidly apart, his ferocious mustache always tilted in a sneer, all served to establish his unquestioned superiority, although I later learned that he could barely read and write. Nevertheless he was God and demanded instant obedience and respect. We had already learned that - he had told us in no uncertain terms as soon as we recruits were delivered like cattle into his gnarled hands.

The Chief never really walked - he swaggered, swinging his arms in long arcs, and literally snarled at the world. It was he we were expected to emulate if we were ever to become sailors in the U.S. Navy.

All those muscles - 120 sets - snapped to various degrees of attention. Apparently the Chief's - and probably the official Navy's - technique to "make men of us" was to treat us as cretins and scum, at least during our boot training. He never spoke except in a growling shout, his eyes darting darkly everywhere, searching for some impropriety among us to magnify into a treasonable offense. While he droned on - if you can use that term for his transparently illiterate snarls at the decibel level of a rock band - I realized that my quivers were gone but my buddies were quaking in their boots. I couldn't maintain much respect for stupidity, no matter where it appeared.

After he finally left, having drilled into us the schedule for the next day, we again fell to, making up our bunks and getting ready for lights out. One by one the guys finished their chores and stripped down, grabbed one of the brand new, white towels from our issued lot, and headed for the showers. The glimpses of hairy crotches and bulging buns that I managed to sneak before they disappeared behind the stark whiteness of the towels set my knees shaking again.

I didn't think I could maintain control in my present state, so I stretched out on the bunk with closed eyes, hoping the quivering in my loins would stop. It seemed to help. Many of the guys were already returning to their bunks, gleaming clean and smelling fresh, when I finally padded to the showers.

The building was double with spaces for two compa-nies, one on each side of the "U" shape, and two shower rooms back to back at the closed end of the "U". The other side of the building was empty, leaving two shower rooms available for us until the next company arrived. We didn't fully appreciate that luxury at the time, not having to wait in line for the shower with all that flesh so close and yet so far. I peered into the first shower room, steamy and noisy, and found it full of guys in various stages of soaping and rinsing. As they rotated under the spray their tantalizing pricks swung and slapped their thighs and soapy water coursed down the crack of their taut asses. My dick gave a lurch, and I hurried on to the next shower room.

There was one empty shower head in the second room, right in the middle. On each side were three guys cavorting companionably, joking and laughing, soaping up their hairy crotches and making squishy sounds with their soap bars in their ass cracks. I stopped uncertainly, not sure I could take that exposure without revealing my excitement.

"Come on in," called one of the guys hospitably. His name was Werner, I remembered, because he was close to me in the alphabetical listing. He was also tall and hairy, handsome in a vaguely sinister way, with uneven teeth. He beckoned to me and there was no choice. I flipped off my towel and snagged it on a rusty nail in the wall, trying not to look where I desperately wanted to look and to will away the embarrassing turgidity between my legs.

The water was shockingly cold at first and adjusted only with some difficulty. I concentrated totally on that tricky valve as long as I could, but realized that even the brief cold shower hadn't had its purported influence on my cock. So much for the therapeutic claims for cold showers. I soaped up, keeping my gaze fixed at the cracked tiles high on the wall and avoiding my crotch, but eventually I had to turn around.

I met several pairs of eyes fleetingly, and then all of them dropped at least momentarily to my cock. That was all it took. The touch of their glances made it rear rigidly, and I quickly turned to the wall again. Gradually the noise level seemed to subside, the conversation became less spontaneous, and then I realized that the guys next to me, Werner on one side and an athletic blond on the other, were also turned to the wall and eyeing my throbbing boner with interest.

"Well, what have we here?" Werner said clearly but in a vaguely threatening tone next to me. There were a couple of chuckles from others, but no one ventured an answer.

"This guy gets a hardon, watching us guys sluicing off," he continued, starting to stroke his own dick. "That right?" he came closer, breathing down my neck.

Flustered, I swung around to avoid him, although the thickening pole in his hands brought all kinds of fantasies to my whirling brain. Unfortunately, in my haste I dropped the soap which slithered toward the drain in the middle of the floor, leaving a smeared trail. I quickly darted after it as if it were my lifesaver. As I stooped to pick it up - you know what happened; I found Werner's thick prick pressed into my ass crack before I could straighten up.

While that may have been one of my fantasies, it couldn't happen like this! I quickly twisted away, only to slip on the soapy trail on the tile floor and land on my ass. My cock stiffly slapped my belly above, not even deterred by the pain in my butt. And immediately I was surrounded by six guys, all with soapy, stiff pricks in their fists and shit-eating grins on their faces.

Werner was by far the most impressive. Although only slightly older than I, he was a city boy and obviously had been around. His body was also more mature, it seemed, with a thick mat of black hair covering his broad chest and narrowing only slightly at the waist before engulfing his crotch. He was straddling my head, and from my position beneath him I could see that even his asshole was ringed with the same black sprigs.

I don't mean that the others weren't enough to explain the throbbing going on between my legs. As I gazed up, my heart in my mouth, the bulging leg muscles, most of them covered liberally with coarse hairs plastered wetly to all that skin, and the spreading chests and shoulders business - and whether they - uh - would be good investments -" He was panting in rhythm with his hand, eyes bulging.

Loverbuns was about to receive his reward.

"I firmly believe in gay liberation -" Richie gritted, grabbing his chair to keep from flying high, and then he liberated about a cup of instant breakfast which Loverbuns gulped down hungrily. Richie thrust upward as he held the boy's head firmly, feeding his face as they both liked it.

A white splash appeared on the bottom of the table across from Richie. Honeyfart quivered and shook violently as splash after splash jetted upward to drip down on Loverbuns' half-naked butt. His cum ran into the pretty ass crack, and Honeyfart responded by stiffening *in extremis*, so to speak.

That did it. The creaky chair finally gave up its herculean task of supporting the mass of quaking blubber, and Honeyfart crashed to the floor on his back, his legs flying up and out. His little sausage sprayed upward a couple of times, the syrup spotting his conservative striped tie in an interesting pattern.

Richie fucked the boy's face until his balls were drained, the wave slowly receding. Then while Loverbuns held his drooping prize tenderly in his mouth, he relaxed and lit a cigarette, quizzically studying Honeyfart struggling on his back like a turtle out of water, his little cock softening quickly in a pudgy paw.

Finally the chairman of several boards of directors managed to roll on his side and struggle to his knees, his eyes still bulging from the strain and his finest orgasm in many years. He managed to grasp the door frame and pulled himself up hand over hand.

"I'll send you a generous retainer," he gasped and staggered out the door, his shrunken peanut still protruding from his gaping fly.

Coming out while wearing a condom
may not seem like the naked truth,
but it's better than the bare facts.

rolling with the movements of their flailing fists, brought on even greater trembling from head to toe. The blond was cradling his balls in his free hand. I dared not touch my own cock; it would only confirm what they seemed to know already. I lay stiffly with fists clenched, not daring to move. The labored breaths of the guys working over me grew louder, becoming low groans issuing from six straining throats. I couldn't meet any of their eyes, but they were intent upon me, that was clear.

The first glob of cum landed on my chest with a splat! Hot and creamy, it spread quickly between my tits and seemed to precipitate several streams of thick gism spurting from as many cocks. When they started to cum, they all drew closer so that not a drop was wasted on the flooding floor. I gasped at the searing heat of each spurt covering me. And then as I looked up again at Werner, he let loose with his thick stream directly into my face, a sardonic grin on his twisted face. It splattered my cheeks and chin and ran into my mouth. It tasted rich and sweet, my first taste of man juice. At that moment my cock jerked and spurted, untouched, covering my belly with its own essence...

I woke suddenly, bathed in a sticky puddle in the bed and panting in joy and terror. The lights were out and I heard the soft snores of the other guys, busy with their own dreams. Quietly I got out of my bunk and washed up in the deserted, brightly-lit shower room, taking the shower I had only dreamed before, with the ghosts of big-pricked sailors all around.

The next two weeks were hurry-up-and-wait, always under the scowling snarls of The Chief. Double-time to class, then double-time to the chow hall for tasteless slop, then back to class and drills in proper military uniforms and etiquette. By the time for lights-out, we were all tired, physically and mentally, and sick to death of the never-ending badgering and watch-standing, which frequently consisted of standing guard over deserted buildings. Few of us responded well to it; the grind seemed to intimidate the timid and merely aggravate the secure. Showering was not that difficult, I found, since by the end of the day we all wanted nothing more than to get to sleep. One time I came upon two guys who were cuming in their fists while watching each other in the shower, but they didn't seem too disturbed that I had witnessed their innocent fun.

Finally the time for our first big (?) weekend liberty arrived - our first opportunity away from the rigid confines of the barracks and discipline of The Chief. Since we had a very limited time (twelve hours) there was no thought of going anywhere except the rather small town near the base. For the first time we donned our dress whites, tied our silly kerchiefs around our necks, and unrolled our white hats, attempting to produce just the right "salty" shape. We all crowded into the tired liberty bus and a short time later streamed onto the civilian streets.

By this time I had struck up a friendship with another sailor who also seemed quiet and out of place. We never talked much, but I knew that Ron was just as miserable as I in that intensely militaristic society. Those of us who were naturally more reticent became almost withdrawn. The more extrovertive types became more aggressive, when they could get away with it. And no matter what the question, the stock answer was "Yes, Sir!", whether it was warranted or not.

Together Ron and I strolled around the town, ate several greasy hamburgers, and pretended to ogle the girls (at least I pretended, I wasn't sure about Ron). When night fell, with only a few free hours left before our return to the base, Ron decided to see a movie (some science fiction thing), but I didn't intend to waste those hours of freedom so simply. So I left him at the theater and started aimlessly down a dark street, relieved to be alone for the first time in weeks.

I heard footsteps behind me but thought nothing of it until they caught up with me. It was Werner.

"Lookin' for something?" he said in his superior way, matching his stride with mine. He had started growing a mustache, and the dark smudge above his upper lip gave him an even more sardonic expression in the dim light. From overhearing his conversations with other sailors, I knew that he had been in a street gang in a major city and had even had a steady girl to fuck whenever he wanted. At least that is what he said. I didn't believe everything he said, of course, but his was a sort of guy I had never met before. By this time I was not as overwhelmed by him as in my dream, but the impact was still there.

"Not really - are you?" I responded as firmly as I could.

"Yeah." His answer was short and mysterious. After a quick glance at me he continued, "And I think I found it. Follow me."

He turned into an alley which was so dark that even the rotting garbage giving off a heady aroma could not be seen. I started to follow and then hesitated. Then I felt his hand on my neck, propelling me forward ahead of him. We stopped in a niche of the old brick building and he pushed me against the wall, leaning toward me ominously.

"Look," he breathed into my face, "I'm used to gettin' my rocks off regular, see? That ain't so easy on the base, right? My fuckin' hand ain't what I got in mind. Instead, I think you got the mouth that would do just fine, with a little instruction, and I intend to make you my private fuck-face. You got that?"

My heart stopped and started up again at twice its former rate. I had never been so insulted or frightened, and I loved it. I had never sucked a cock, but I also knew I would love that. For the two weeks or so since my dream, I had toyed with various ideas about how I was going to find out what man sex was all about, especially in the Navy. Werner's arrogant proprietorship was just what I needed. My cock stiffened quickly in my pants.

"Yes, sir," I said automatically, gulping nervously. I meant it that time.

I guess my immediate acquiescence startled him. He had expected resistance, perhaps even a back-alley fight which he would surely win. He stared at me in the gloom, perhaps suspecting a trick. He could only have seen a trembling excitement in my face.

He groped my crotch and immediately encountered an obvious hard-on. He grunted. "Take it out," he commanded. In a moment my boner was stabbing the cool night air. Again he grunted. "That's what I thought," he muttered confidently.

He began to fumble with his fly, and I wished for more light. I wanted to see that enormous prick as in my dream, but no chance. Instead he fished it out and pushed me to my knees, rubbing it in my face. It was warm and thick, becoming harder by the second.

"Open up, and watch the teeth." I obeyed, thrilling to the spongy, bulbous head entering my mouth. He stopped at that point, apparently experienced in training first-timers, I thought. I learned I could breathe around it but most of the time I forgot to breathe, raptly savoring it. But then after a few moments he pushed further in, spreading my lips and filling my throat.

"Uh," he grunted softly, not pressing but just enjoying. I could taste a sweetness, and ventured to move my tongue from side to side to enhance it. The movement brought out his lust, and he shoved the entire tool in to the hairy root.

I gagged, and he withdrew, again hissing, "Watch the

fuckin' teeth!" Again he pressed forward, and I managed to breathe through my nose as he filled me with his meat. "Oh, shit, yeah!" he moaned, his cock lurching and swelling. Quickly he unfastened his white pants and let them drop, and I hesitantly reached for the hairy balls hanging heavily between his legs.

"Yeah, grab my nuts," he ordered, his breaths coming short and rasping. I thrilled to their size and potency, like a man-bull, I thought deliriously. I even ran my finger back toward his asshole, encountering those crisp, dark hairs that I had seen in my dream.

I could feel his knees bending under the pressure of my amateurish love-making, and I knew this was where I belonged. It gave me a feeling of power that I could bring such a man to the pinnacle of passion, and I redoubled my frantic efforts on his cock, shielding my teeth with my lips. I could feel his legs begin to tremble like mine were.

"Take it all!" he moaned, shoving me hard against the brick wall. I gasped for breath, but he was beyond gentleness. He plowed my aching jaws twice more before stiffening and letting loose his volley of cum, just like in my dream. I couldn't see it this time, but I tasted every drop - sweet, spicy, and rich, just as I had imagined. I gulped it down thirstily with no hesitation.

I think he was still cuming when he roughly pulled me to my feet and found my threatening prick. He gripped it hard and gave a twist, and I shot all over his hand and the cluttered alley.

That was the first of many cums we shared during the weeks of boot camp. Late at night in the shower, in a deserted barracks that one of us had been assigned to "guard", in the shadow of a "dumpster" on moonless nights, whenever he felt the urge.

He liked to pretend he was forcing me to suck him off, and I enjoyed the fantasy. I loved him when he swaggered, like The Chief, and shoved my face down on his bone. He never failed to jerk me off as well, and in reflection I think he enjoyed that as much as I did. One weekend we rented a hotel room and I persuaded him to jack off on my face in the shower. But this time I felt cheated that I wasn't able to swallow it all, and we never repeated that scene. We lost track of each other when we graduated and were sent to different duty stations.

Now it's my turn, a successful professional many years later, to swagger in my own way, to teach young men the fine art of servicing. But there's no place like Boot Camp to bring out the slave in a man.

THE END

RICHIE RAMMER

The feathery touch started at his toes and moved slowly upward, and by the time it approached his crotch, he was ready. It had become a morning ritual, the only way to start the day for Richie Rammer, stud *extraordinaire*. As a free-lance writer he was good - but as a fucker he was great! He would be the first to tell you, but a lot of testimonials were available on request as well.

Without opening his eyes, he placed a hand on the bulge moving under the sheet. It felt like a spherical shoe brush and never ceased to amuse him - a butch haircut kept about an inch long on top of a compact muscular body containing a brain that was all gay. But the haircut was not an important element in Loverbuns' list of attributes. His long, pink tongue and his twitching asshole were what really mattered, as well as his insatiable appetite for hard dick which Richie always had plenty of.

The moist tingle was circling the throbbing tower like a carnivorous animal. The mammoth meat would be a several course meal since there hadn't been any action for over twelve hours, about the maximum time span Richie allowed between episodes. Beyond twelve hours his ears began to buzz, his fingers twitched, his muscles hunched, and his perpetual erection was a hazard to ordinary clothes. He could always depend on Loverbuns (his real name was Elmer) to use his key in the morning to wake him properly.

He spread his legs sleepily and the punk man-servant grasped the opportunity to latch onto his huge balls, now resting tranquilly on the bed but poised to go. He knew where his breakfast was coming from! He proceeded to heat up his food in a wet mouth, with the velvet tongue titillating the hairy sack.

Slowly awakening, Richie lifted his knees and spread them wide. Loverbuns crawled all the way under the sheet, stretching out between his sleepy boss' hairy, muscle-strapped legs, hungry for raunchy Richie. His tongue tip moved down from his balls, suggesting a lower liaison, and Richie was in favor. He rolled his hips up and presented his asshole for some of the same treatment.

The tongue lapped the tense muscle and then stiffened and darted inside. Three hot licks and he was ready to fire. Briefly he squeezed his legs together, trapping the bristly head between his thighs, but the tongue continued to probe and thrust, sending the mercury higher. The fluttering fingers on his furry fuckballs didn't serve to cool him off much either. He was in no condition for leisurely lovemaking this morning!

Richie's ramrod sent signals threatening explosion. We'll do the next one slower, he promised himself. He took Loverbuns' sheet-shrouded head between his hands and held it over the pulsing pole, posed for a powerdive. Then he shoved it down firmly.

"Eat it, man," he growled, and felt the hot mouth enclose the throbbing head, nibbling it gently between his pure white choppers.

"Oh, shit," he groaned, body rigid from that painful joy, or the joyful pain, that Loverbuns could always produce. The velvet tongue swirled around the ridge and the flaring head swelled even more, filling his avid aperture. Between the tongue and the teeth the treatment was terrific, and Richie's toes began to curl.

"Take it, cocksucker," he gritted. That was a very tall order. Loverbuns' breakfast was a thick ten inches of rigid prick, straight and pointing toward heaven as did his eyes when he descended all the way. Every gay guy reacted the same, as Richie had first discovered when he was about fourteen years old. They had all gagged and squealed, but they all loved it and begged for more as often as he would allow. And Richie was very generous; he believed in spreading his wealth broadly.

Loverbuns sucked hard as he slurped up and down. He knew Richie couldn't take much of that without firing one volley, and he was hungry. One hand slid down to caress his own cock pressed hard against the bed as he felt Richie tense.

Richie moved his foot up to the rounded ass that had suggested his *nom de guerre*, working a horny toe into the greased asshole under the sheet. It was hot and wet, and he wriggled his big toe into the feverish pit as a bonus for the good work. With his eyes still closed, Richie thrust upward into the tongue-twirling tunnel. Loverbuns murmured and moaned, turned on by the big toe and the even bigger invading monster. Richie poised on the brink, the floodgate set to open when he gave the nod.

"You're a hungry bitch," Richie began talking to him in gutter growls, knowing he liked that. "Sucking cock for breakfast, Loverbuns - get your high protein diet, bitch - slurp it up - "

Loverbuns started to convulse under the sheet, loving the insolence of his master with his monster meat, needing the impending powerful pulses, alternating current for his purring asshole motor. He burbled as his own vibrations became shudders of joy and he started to spurt onto the sheet with a shaking spasm.

Right on schedule, Richie filled his mouth with his juice course, creamy cum which was gulped down thirstily, the man's toe shoved deep into his avid asshole. Then Richie shoved him down on the meat course, all ten inches of throbbing red-blooded gristle, and that's when he choked, but deliciously. The huge prick gushed ropes of joyjuice fit for the king who produced it.

Loverbuns gurgled happily and took it all. Richie finally sighed, equilibrium established again and ready for a new day.

135

Loverbuns let it soak until Richie started to worry about the oxygen supply under the sheet. Besides, he was getting hungry! He flipped back the cover, exposing the tanned, blond, muscular form bent double over his crotch. He liked that view, and Loverbuns sighted up at him over his favorite landscape, the flat, ridged belly and broad hairy chest of his favorite satyr. Richie's luxurious brown mustache was cocked at an angle from his sardonic grin. The cocksucker slowly released the drained cock.

"Good morning," he murmured, licking his lips like a cat to get the last traces of cream. "Hungry?"

"That's right, Loverbuns," Richie replied indulgently. "You've already eaten but I'm still starved. I'll brush the ivories while you rustle something up, right?"

Loverbuns hopped out of bed promptly, his rounded buns flashing and beckoning as he bent to retrieve his scanty clothes. Richie reached for those mouthwatering mounds, but Loverbuns giggled out of reach and dashed into the kitchen.

A half hour later they were both seated at the glass breakfast table, Richie in a short terrycloth robe, reading the paper and trying to eat bacon and eggs - trying, because Loverbuns' cock and balls were protruding lewdly from the leg of the short-short cutoffs clearly visible through the table.

In the "Times" there was a review of his latest documentary, a treatise on the love lives of the Himalayan monks, and as usual the remarks were both pro and con. Godfrey Galapodopoulis sneered that "Mr. Rammer must have been hidden under the robes of the monks to get the worm's eye view", but Gloria Rockum gushed about "Mr. Rammer's exquisite sensitivity to the tender traces of femininity in the seclusive aesthetes". "Aesthetes" is right, Richie grunted; they liked aesthetic cocks rammed up their aesthetic asses best of all!

When Loverbuns saw that the boss was determined

to read the paper, he crawled under the table and began giving head slowly, mostly lips and tongue. Richie grunted again, more happily this time, and spread his legs. Loverbuns loosened Richie's short robe so he could caress his hairy belly and chest. Richie watched for a moment through the glass, his restiffened rod throbbing between the pink lips. Then he settled down to a long dissertation on the progress on new companies in interesting serious investors while Loverbuns took care of the stiff competition. But then the doorbell rang.

"Get that, will you, baby?" Richie asked absently, only vaguely aware of the interruption. His cock bobbed stiff and wet and cool when the mouth left it. In a minute Loverbuns returned with a red-faced beefy man in tow.

"Mr. Rammer?" a hoarse, raspy voice quavered from the doorway.

Richie looked up briefly, registered a quick dislike, muttered "Yes," and went back to his paper.

The thick bifocals glittered as the visitor waddled toward the table, puffing from the minimal exertion. Loverbuns wrinkled his nose is distaste behind him, but Richie tried to ignore it. He resignedly dropped the paper on the table in front of him.

"Allow me to introduce myself," the visitor wheezed, placing a card on the table. "I am Maxwell Honeyfart the Third. I suppose you may have heard of me. I am on the board of directors of a few - uh - rather substantial businesses, blue chips, as it were - ahem."

Honeyfart's head kept tipping up and down as he tried to focus his glasses on the writer's face, but with only moderate success. A spotted, pudgy paw was held out over the table generally in Richie's direction.

Richie toyed with the idea of ignoring the interruption entirely but thought better of it. He had heard of Honeyfart from the business pages and, although he hadn't the slightest idea what the man wanted, had to admit that he had no prospects at the moment for another article or series to pay the rent, and maybe this creep could be talked out of a few schekels along those lines.

He forced a tolerant smile to his face and grasped the slimy palm long enough to pass for a handshake. He gestured to the chair across the table that Loverbuns had just vacated. This put the slob at a low level so he had even more difficulty with the angle of his bifocals.

"So what can I do for you, Mr. Honey - ahem - fart?" Loverbuns giggled and Richie tried to give him a stern look.

Honeyfart cleared his throat again, his eyes fixed on the paper spread out before Richie.

"I see you are reading the business section of the 'Times'. It so happens my subject is introduced by that article on new investments," he finally wheezed.

Richie retrieved the paper, trying to ignore Loverbuns who was frantically pointing at Richie's exposed crotch. As he picked up the paper the subject crotch with its waving flag came into clear view. This was too much of a temptation for Loverbuns.

"You mean this article about growing companies with sharp management teams?"

Honeyfart adjusted and readjusted his glasses, trying to focus on the object that somehow seemed out of place, that bobbing pinkish pole under the glass table. He stared in shock as he identified the hairy crotch and towering tool.

"Ah, yes, ah - I beg your pardon - ah - excuse me, I mean - "

Loverbuns had decided to ignore the fat flab and crawled under the table again, assuming his favorite position even though it meant crawling over shiny patent leather shoes to get at that masterful meat. His curvy buns pointed at Honeyfart, and if he could have focused on them, the pudgy pachyderm could have seen the boy's cock and balls escaping from his shorts, as usual.

Honeyfart's eyes began to bulge and his head tilted up and down frantically as he tried to determine what the crew-cut blond was doing. He finally got focused again on Richie's stiff prick pointing skyward, nearly touching the table in its tumescence, but then it disappeared between the pink pouting lips.

Richie reread the introduction to the article. He didn't see anything about Honeyfart of any of his usual companions.

"How does the article concern you?" he asked brusquely, wanting to get rid of him as soon a possible so he could get back to more important matters, like plugging Loverbuns' nether regions.

"Uh, what?" Honeyfart was squirming as he stared at the fascinating fellatio. His chair squeaked threateningly as he wriggled.

"I said, what is your connection with these growing companies?" Richie was becoming impatient.

"Oh, ah - " Honeyfart moped his dripping brow, trying to maintain some vestige of decorum. "Yes - ah - I also have interests in an investment group and - ah - you see - ah -"

Apparently Honeyfart's thoughts were interrupted because Loverbuns was sucking the big balls and stroking the stiff staff with both hands, and even Richie was distracted by that blissful treatment.

Unconsciously the fat financier began to diddle himself under the pendulous paunch that seemed to be contained only by the vest stretched across it. He was hypnotized by the scene under the table.

"An investment group?" Richie prodded, a little breathless himself.

"Uh - yes. Gays have a way - a marvelous way - of - doing things - uh - differently - uh - sometimes surprisingly - uh -"

139

"Gays? What does this article have to do with gays?" Richie tensed despite his attempt to remain composed.

"What? Oh - uh - " Honeyfart was gripping a tiny tidbit in his crotch, his eyes fixed on the action. Loverbuns returned to the rampant rod but continued to stroke the wet balls and finger the sensitive spot below the sack. His fingertips almost touched Richie's asshole that was beginning to tingle in warning.

"Some of these companies are run entirely by gays, and it is doubtful if they can - uh - do their business - that is - along with their other interests - uh - although I'm sure some of them are - uh - very talented - "

Loverbuns was showing his talent now in the extent he was able to swallow that huge shaft. He took great pride in his deepthroat technique, and he really needed it with Richie, the original super-challenge. His shorts had slipped down exposing his ass crack, and Honeyfart began to drool when he was able to focus on those bulging buns.

"So how do I fit into this?" Richie asked impatiently, his balls beginning to churn as the tantalizing tongue rasped along the underside of his rampant rod.

"You are an - uh - investigative reporter - uh - and have a reputation for - uh - relating to gays -" Honeyfart was even more breathless. "You can name your price -" He was squirming and twisting, the red head of his little sausage clearly visible in his fist and threatening to boil over.

"You want me to interview them, or do some article on these gay-owned companies?" Richie was beginning to breathe heavily also, approaching the edge of the cliff. He was annoyed at the impertinence of the man to play with his knob in Richie's kitchen, but the tingle in his own asshole - a sure sign of impending flood - was becoming a full-blown surge.

"Yes, find out how - competent they are - uh - in

140

Richie pulled Loverbuns from under the table by the waistband of his shorts, completing the job of exposing those famous globes. That was enough to bring renewed life to his still-dripping cock.

"Come on, Loverbuns, I'm going to fuck your ass and then you can pack my bags. I've got a job to do in San Francisco!"

*　*　*

"Uh - don't you have to - uh - carry some bags or something?" Richie asked when his stomach growled for the second time.

The tall, muscular bellhop still didn't seem to hear. He continued to sit dreamily on Richie's crotch, shifting slightly back and forth and rotating in small circles, Richie's recently-drained cock still filling his ass very satisfyingly, it seemed.

"Ummm?" the bellman responded, his green eyes flashing open for a moment like a "Go" traffic signal before resuming their trance. "Oh, that's all right. My father owns the hotel, you know. I only work when I feel like it, and because I look sexy in the uniform. Ummm, so big and fat and still hard - "

Never let it be said that Richie turned down a handsome trick like this one, but this had been going on more or less steadily since last night when he had checked into the hotel fresh off the plane. When the bellman stooped to deposit his bags in his room he had just kept going in that direction, nuzzling the ever-present bulge in the newest guest's crotch. Aside from snatching a couple of hours sleep here and there during the night, it had been a semi-continuous scene ever since.

"You - sort of go with the room, is that it?"

"We're a CSGB establishment, you know, and Dad says it's good for business," he murmured, his firm buns compressing the thick stalk rhythmically. "Business" - that reminded Richie of the reason for his being in San Francisco in the first place. With a quick twist Richie flipped the boy on his back under him and gave a deep thrust for good measure. That elicited a quick gasp and a twitch to the cock riding on the lean belly. His mother, a former vaudeville trooper, had taught him the old cliche, "always leave them begging for more", and Richie usually followed her advice.

"I'm hungry and I've got things to do today, kid," he explained as his cock popped free and he padded his way naked toward the bathroom. "Bring me up some bacon and eggs, if you're still in the bellman business," glancing briefly at the crestfallen face of his latest admirer. "And a newspaper," he added, closing the bathroom door firmly. When he emerged later his breakfast was neatly arranged on the table and a newspaper propped against the orange juice glass. There was also a phone number plainly evident, scrawled across the front page.

As he ate, Richie compared the advertisements he found in the paper with a list of businesses he had brought with him, gleaned from his research into gay-owned businesses in the Bay Area. An hour later he sauntered into one of them, a clothing store called "Bodyforms" on Castro Street. Outside he noticed a discrete sign, "CSGB", the same acronym used by the bellman. He would have to inquire about that, he decided.

Even at the early hour, the store was busy with shoppers. Some were gay men, but there were almost as many women, mostly well-dressed and even matronly. The assortment of clothes was not exactly conventional, ranging from collegiate jackets to bikinis, from leather pants, chaps, and jackets to frilly red and black undies that would have made even his mother blush. He observed the action for a few minutes, especially the attentive assistance provided by the young, handsome clerks who covered the store thoroughly.

Richie was drawn by the leather pants and picked out a pair he thought would fit. A clerk glided up and directed him to the changing rooms at the rear of the store. "Booth C should be just right for you," the clerk murmured.

When Richie pushed aside the curtain as directed, he was astonished by the size of the area. Lit dimly, the large room contained at least ten booths with doors draped in black leather. In the hall between the two rows of booths a slim boy with a very hairy chest was modeling a red net corselet with narrow straps over the shoulders and ending in fringe at the bottom that didn't come close to covering a prominent jockstrap bulge.

"Oh, yes, that's lovely," an overweight matron was exclaiming, her eyes fixed on the crotch and ignoring the rest.

The model turned on his matching high red heels in the best courtesan manner, exposing two prime buns adorned only with the strap up the middle and red fringe.

"I think my husband will like that," the woman gushed. "Don't you think so?"

Any guy with taste would appreciate that pretty ass, Richie thought. He watched as the woman began to finger the fringe, and as the boy turned around again, her fingertips drifted across the bulging basket.

"Maybe we should go into the booth if you wish to examine the merchandise more closely," the boy cautioned, a bored look on his face. They disappeared into a cubicle and Richie found Booth C as suggested.

The back wall of the booth was mirrored, but the side walls were merely lattices with three inch gaps between diagonal slats of smooth redwood. The side walls were only about four feet apart. With such large gaps the walls were more minor obstacles to familiarity than separations.

They certainly didn't effectively isolate Richie from the hunky blond football-type in a garish numbered sports jersey checking his reflection on one side, or the slender-muscled black young man trying on successions of matching jockstraps and tennis shorts in Booth B. A tennis racket leaned against the wall on the other side.

As soon as Richie entered the booth he was aware of abrupt cessation of activity in both booths B and D. Both sets of eyes roamed over him, their potential purchases ignored for the moment. The hunky one, after a quick check, removed his sneakers and pants, apparently in order to evaluate the jersey better. He stood near the mirror for a moment, fluffing his considerable and growing dick, and then turned a plumb, rounded rear toward Richie, pretending to be surveying the effect of the jersey.

Richie began undressing to try on the leather properly while keeping his eyes peeled on his neighbors as well. The black boy seemed to lose interest in the tennis togs, but stood swinging his nude hips in front of the mirror, his long, dangling cock swinging in wide arcs. As he swung the slim, dark muscle grew in length, inch after inch, until it reached at least half-way to his knees, and it was still growing.

Richie straightened up, divested of coverings, and both sets of eyes lit up like neons as they feasted on Richie's meat and potatoes just in time for brunch. Immediately both his neighbors fell to their knees at the intervening walls, and Richie had barely started to warm up. Quickly, under the intense gaze of his devoted subjects, his huge prick stood tall and proud, undaunted by its all-night worship but with the usual dilemma, which way to bestow its favors first. The blond was audibly panting hungrily, but the black stud won the day by reeling out a pointed, pink tongue almost as long as his dick. Richie turned toward him and shoved his entire tool through the latticed wall and down the hot, churning throat.

Richie's muscles snapped in awe of the skill and consummate lust of that dark cavern. True to its billing, that long tongue wrapped around him and seemed to cram every inch of his cock deeply into the welcoming craw, and began to lap his hairy balls below for good measure. His throat muscles worked spasmodically around the cockhead, and Richie was soon quivering and thrusting from the exemplary service. Recognizing that sweeping tide already threatening in his balls, Richie pulled back gasping, promising to return for more. It wouldn't be fair to deprive the hungry football hunk who obviously needed some nourishment as well.

When he turned to the other wall there had been a change of scene; instead of a drooling mouth there was a winking asshole begging for an infusion. Richie shrugged; both routes led to the same satiety center. He unhesitatingly shoved his already slick dick into that welcoming asshole that pleaded for sustenance.

Clasping heat swallowed him greedily, the circular stoma like toothless gums sucking him inside. The firm, tanned buns pressed against the perforated wall, and Richie pressed in balls-deep, his cream already rising to the top. When that masculine ass began to circle and swirl, Richie's teeth began to grate, his own appetite on the upswing.

He glanced over his shoulder to see that enormously long, dark dick dangling through the wall. He reached back to grasp it and his fist was full of throbbing muscle as long as a tennis racket handle, it seemed. For an instant Richie thought perhaps it *was* a racket handle, but when it spewed precum over his hand he decided against that. He slithered and volleyed the hot, silky skin along the foot-long shaft as he tackled the line-backer on the other side. It was already fourth down and the goal was in sight.

146

Richie lost the contest, but his balls won. Up, out, and over the goal posts they soared, sending their surging signals in a fluid arc into the hot receiver. Richie lost track of the tennis player for a moment, his fists gripping his balls to keep them from following the same parabola. It was man against muscle and muscle against man, balls in the air and up the ass. The hunks' pass was grounded in a messy splat between his feet.

Eventually Richie took a breather, retreating to the line of scrimmage as it were, but his dick was still alert and calling the signals. He turned back to the tennis player who had his own game going. Bent over, his ass next to the wall, he was patiently pressing with fingertips his own cock into his asshole as Richie watched, fascinated. First the head disappeared up that brown pucker, and then slowly, an inch and then another inch eased in. His heavy balls were separated widely by the shaft but looked like they might follow it in. Clearly this guy was an ace.

"Singles" was only an expression, Richie decided; "doubles" were better. In a moment his own cock was shoving in alongside the black one, his two white balls nudging the black ones indiscriminately. The two cockheads kissed in passing, their velvet ridges riding close and matching point for point. In and out he moved, each time returning the volley and reaching for greater distance.

Richie could feel that thick cock swell and throb against his; for the tennis player it was a combination of fucking and being fucked simultaneously, and his strings sang with each service. Only a few volleys later the boy groaned and Richie could feel the hot cum drench the channel and flood his own cock thrusting deep, and he met the challenge, adding his own thick streams in set point. Nobody lost that match.

About five minutes later, Richie, somewhat weak in the knees, walked to the check-out counter wearing the black leather pants he had managed to squeeze into. "Beautiful," breathed the handsome clerk, his eyes fixed on the enormous bulge down one leg. "You'll take it, I assume?"

"I give it more often than take it," Richie responded with a stern stare, but then broke into a smile at the delicate shiver that shook the clerk deliciously.

"By the way," he asked as the clerk was making change, "what does CSGB mean on the sign out front?"

"Oh," the clerk smiled. "It is the secret of our success, we think, as well as most of the establishments in the Castro. "It stands for 'Cock Sucking is Good Business', of course. Didn't you know?"

THE END

LESSON IN SEX

The warm, spring sun slanted through the high windows in the long hallway leading to the lecture rooms of Cal-Tech Mens College. The other students buzzed and brushed by on their way to classes or a respite in the sun as Rod paused to check the notice outside Room 69.

```
          SAFE SEX
           TODAY

    REQUIRED FOR GRADUATION!
```

Rod's dark mustache lifted with his smile at implications of the terse announcement. Hell, almost any sex would be welcome, graduation or not! In fact, perhaps in response to the budding spring outside, his juices were really flowing these days, he thought, his levis tight around his muscular thighs and rounded butt. A close look at his packed crotch could have detected a tiny twitch as the thought of sex intruded on the more mundane subjects of primary concern those last few weeks before cap-and-gown time.

What the announcement should have said was that, because of AIDS and the increasing transmission of the virus among college students, the school had decreed that all students must receive two hours of classroom instruction on transmission routes and risk reduction before they could graduate. Rod had to admit that he really didn't know much about it except for some scary reports about guys, mostly gays, dying of AIDS in San Francisco and a couple of kids kept out of school because of it. Since he wasn't exactly in the "fast lane", he hadn't really thought much about it. He commuted from home to school and worked part-time in a grocery store, which didn't leave much time for playing around.

He blushed slightly thinking of the time a few weeks ago when the night manager in the store had grabbed him at the urinal and given him a quick blow-job after the store shelves had been stocked for the night. His hot mouth and lashing tongue had been a revelation, but he had avoided the kind of greasy guy ever since.

A student brushed by, his hand trailing for a brief lingering moment on his ass. Rod looked quickly as the figure passed on his way into the lecture room. A really neat blond guy with short, spiky hair, a trim lithe figure in white shorts, and almost lavender eyes that sparkled back in a quick grin over his shoulder. Rod had noticed him before - he thought his name was Jerry - and had thought that maybe he was gay. Rod didn't really know much about that. Other than a few brief and confusing contacts with girls in the family car at the drive-in and petting sessions after school dances, he wasn't that experienced. It really wasn't all that great. He had had a few jack-off sessions with a buddy in high school while they looked at nude pictures in magazines, and he sometimes got a partial erection in the gym locker room, but he guessed that was normal.

At that point the lecturer arrived, so Rod took a seat about half-way back. Only after he sat down did he notice that Jerry was sitting right next to him. The lavender eyes took in the rangy frame, the dark, curly hair needing a comb, and the wisps of dark chest hair curling over his T-shirt neck. Rod nodded but kept his attention on the teacher who was beginning his talk.

All those statistics - mostly gay men, many of them in their twenties (Rod had just turned 21), dead or dying from infections after exposure to a queer-looking virus with bumps on it in the diagram. Pictures of guys with purple spots all over them, looking like victims of prisoner of war camps only months after climbing mountains in apparent good health. Everybody was deadly serious in the class as those grim facts were brought out.

Rod glanced at Jerry who was staring at the instructor with a fixed expression. His eyes seemed moist as if he might cry. Maybe he knew someone who had AIDS. Rod looked away quickly, not wanting to see that look on that handsome face.

Then the instructor started to talk about the ways the virus got around, and for the first time seemed a little uncomfortable with his subject. Rod could see he really didn't want to use four-letter words, but the long involved terms, like anal intercourse and oral-genital contact, didn't seem to come off very well. And what was oral-anal contact anyway - Rod hadn't had any experience along that line.

"He means rimming," Jerry whispered to him, their first actual verbal contact. "Oh," Rod whispered back uncertainly - rimming?

He noticed that Jerry's muscular legs were covered with soft, downy blond fur, perhaps bleached by the sun that had tanned him well above the level of his brief shorts. Rod blushed again, thinking of what might be above, especially since the shorts seemed awfully full in the crotch. He wrenched his attention back to the lecture.

"Sharing needles is the second most dangerous activity," the lecturer was saying. "Don't use intravenous drugs, but if you must, at least clean them in bleach between uses."

Rod had had no experience along that line either, but was familiar with the scenes in the alleys near the bus station where he assumed that sort of thing went on.

"AIDS is not a gay disease. It is also transmitted during heterosexual intercourse, and in both directions."

This statement brought on more restless shuffling in

151

the students than any previous points he had made. Rod looked around at some of the notorious "studs" who looked really worried for the first time. Rod didn't have to worry about that much with his rotten sex life! And then the teacher showed some pictures of babies with AIDS, looking something like the pictures of starving kids in Africa. The room was totally silent.

"As I said before, AIDS is not a gay disease but because it affects so many gay men, we should discuss the homosexual lifestyle." Again the instructor seemed uneasy about his subject, and a few students snickered. Both Rod and Jerry stared straight ahead, avoiding each other's eyes.

The instructor rambled on, saying that psychiatrists said it was an "alternative" to straight, family-oriented society, and that love and intimacy were not restricted to marriage and child-raising. When he finished his subject, Rod was no less confused about his own feelings than before, but at least the teacher hadn't said it was immoral or nasty or anything like that. It was just - different.

He tried not to look at Jerry, but caught a wry look for a second before the end of the class. "Tomorrow at the same time, gentlemen," the instructor said and walked out without asking for questions, appearing relieved that the hour was over.

As they both stood up to leave, Jerry smiled, "See you tomorrow, Rod," and left the room. Rod followed more slowly, wondering how Jerry had known his name. He also noticed the trim buns shifting seductively as the blond figure disappeared out the door.

The next day as Rod entered the lecture room there was a bowl full of foil-wrapped articles on the front desk and a sign reading "TAKE ONE ONLY". He picked one up and looked it over curiously. In small print the label said "Condom". Rod had never used one, but had heard stories about how terrible they were. How they slipped off at the wrong time if you managed to get them on without losing your mood. He carried one back to the same seat he had occupied the previous day to look it over.

Just before the lecturer arrived, Jerry squeezed into the seat next to him, seeming a little breathless and holding his condom. "Hi," he smiled. "Your brand?", indicating the foil package.

Rod looked confused, but noticed the tight blue shorts that matched the twinkling eyes and the bulging biceps stretching the short sleeves of his alligator shirt.

"Today we will cover the use of prevention methods. Although the most sure-fire way to avoid AIDS is abstinence, we know that guys your age are not likely to keep it in your pants all the time." Snickers around the room. "Of course masturbation is safe. The next best way is to use a condom." Groans from a few of the more experienced "studs".

"We have a video tape to demonstrate the proper application, and I want you to open the package as you watch, to become more familiar with the technique as we watch the video." The lights were switched off and the large screen at the front of the room was flooded with a picture of a condom. Rod and Jerry tore the wrappers open and extracted the strange circles of rolled plastic as the video demonstrated.

The picture dissolved to a penis - a large, stiff one bobbing from a dark, hairy crotch. There were gasps and giggles all around the room, and Rod almost jumped from the shock of the picture, the organ much larger than life size, obviously ready for almost anything.

He heard Jerry murmur, "Ummmm," and looked quickly at him. Jerry smiled back broadly and then returned his gaze to the screen, obviously fascinated. Rod felt the beginnings of a swelling in his levis.

"You can use two fingers to simulate putting on the condom as you watch the video," the instructor suggested.

153

The next scene was a hand holding the condom and starting to unroll it while grasping the end with the other hand. Rod followed suit. Again he stole a look at Jerry, but Jerry still appeared entranced by the picture. He couldn't help noticing that his crotch was bulging strongly in the blue shorts.

The video hand placed the condom on the head of the huge penis and started to roll it down slowly. Rod used two fingers as instructed, feeling the rather sticky plastic cool and not at all forbidding. His crotch was bulging and throbbing, but he was not sure of the real cause for the excitement.

He glanced at Jerry and then did a double-take. At the cuff of his shorts the bulging pink head of his cock was showing, slowly extending further down his leg as Rod watched. Jerry held the condom still unrolled, his gaze locked on the screen. Rod was glad he had worn levis; if he had worn shorts his own equipment would have shown as Jerry's was. He couldn't take his eyes off that entrancing sight next to him.

Suddenly Jerry noticed Rod looking at him and at the revelation in his crotch. He blushed, starting to recover, but then, sure that Rod was watching, spread his legs even further to show even more of himself. Rod almost fell out of his chair as the sight enlarged. The broad head was almost purple with congestion, and big veins ran tortuously up the shaft. Then with a giggle, Jerry clamped his legs together and tucked it back in with considerable difficulty..

By this time the video operation had been completed, the organ completely sheathed in plastic. Rod hurriedly rolled the condom down over his fingers and tried to listen to the instructions about removal without spilling the contents.

The rest of the lecture passed by Rod's head which was in a fog. He couldn't lose his erection, thinking of

Jerry's throbbing manhood so close and yet so far. When the lecture was finally over and he rose, his bulge was obvious, especially to Jerry whose gaze lingered there.

Rod hurried to the front of the room and discarded the condom in the waste basket as instructed. Jerry was close behind, but before he left he snagged two more condoms from the bowl.

Rod started down the hall, his classes over for the day, and discovered Jerry beside him. His hand touched Rod's as if by accident.

"Mind if I tag along?" Jerry asked quietly.

Rod's brain whirled and he looked into those lavender eyes directly for the first time. There was a mixture of admiration and a certain pleading there, and he felt a sudden thickness, a warmth in his chest. "No, I don't mind," he finally managed to stammer.

They walked for a few moments in silence, out the front door and into the bright sunshine. Simultaneously they stopped after a moment and stood facing each other.

Jerry held up the fresh condoms. "I think we need more experience with these things, don't you?" A tiny smile curved his lips.

It was a moment of silence, of decision. Then they both smiled broadly, turned, and walked together down the path.

THE END

A STORY OF MY LIFE

My life moves from orgasm to orgasm.

The thrill, the quickening pulse, the peristaltic peregrinations from life to death, almost, and then again to life, blissful and serene. A taste of death each time, only to find life again at its sweetest, most triumphant, having survived the challenge and returned victorious.

The ominous rumbling sets my teeth on edge, knowing the moment is at hand. The growls start in my throat, unheard. My muscles stretch and twist, lock in extreme positions. The thunder in my head gives rise to flashes of fire, lightening to the rigid rod clasped in its urgent embrace, signals to take the leap without thought of return or consequence. The pressure builds under his skilled tutilage, he who has taken the trip before and knows every turning, every route to that ultimate destination where life begins and sometimes ends. Still he persists and I acquiese gladly, feeling the earth crumbling under my feet. Then I am over the edge, the precipice abrupt and the pit yawning below, promising nothing but impossible to resist. I scream in joy and release from earthly fetters, my brain blank as a page but instinctively in tune with the nature of man, all men primal and polyandrous. Only man can catapult me, the trajectory that of a waterfall, matching my own emission that is laden with life and lust for the man who pulls the switch.

The landing is gentle, a feathery berth for my snapping joints, a soothing caress for my fevered threshings. I jerk once, twice, perhaps yearning for another flight, even just a short one, but it is not to be. My racing pulse bounds through my head but already it is quieting, and I know it is over until the next time - the next time I am destined to live again for a fleeting moment in that violet void between heaven and earth.

He knows. He understands. He almost flies with me in that joyous journey because he knows the way - not exactly my way but his way is not so different. It is his hands, his lips, his colonic soul that push me over the edge, knowing that I will survive, knowing I need it to survive, and he will be there with me, smiling into my eyes as my senses clear and my teeth unclench. His eyes speak to mine with clarity of love even if we have just met, because he knows, he understands.

All the accountrements are only single stones on the altar for worship of the almighty orgasm. The scenes we manufacture, the props we contrive, the elaborate settings of candlelight and flowers, music and beat, the obedience to fetishes sophisticated and primeval, are merely sprigs of greenery for the ultimate single flower whose bloom bursts with crimson and sprays white seed to the winds.

He waits for me, impatient but concealing it. He also wants to travel that route to oblivion, to experience his own freedom from earthly ties at my hands, my invention for his excursion into space beyond reality. I know. I understand.

I am an organist, master of a mighty instrument. Freshly free of gravity myself, I instinctively release his bonds, bit by bit, link by link, through adagio passages of an unchaining melody. My fingers develop a tripping theme on tender skin just below the fountainhead until I hear a responsive hiss. My lips strike a soft chord on his pendulous orbs, and the duet begins. I feel him tense and his groin pulse quickens. The melody builds, the baritone prominent. There are no female voices in this song. My tongue brings out the basics as it proceeds downward in orderly progression, and his legs lift reflexly as I approach the hidden core, the sweet portal of his inner being.

By combining my hands and tongue, I gradually bring the organ to full resonance, the crescendo building slowly. Probing deeper, I perform modulations that twist the tune from major to minor to major as I play on his body, my organ of which I am master. It obeys my most subtle commands, and his gasps and groans are a counterpoint to my composition. I feel the trembling begin, and know what chords are most productive for the symphony to come. I feel his essence on my drumming fingertips even as I taste his innocence on my tongue. It is time for the final movement.

I, the organist, am in full control, one finger on the pulse beat, one hand grasping his testicles, my lips and tongue teasing him toward the crest of the crescendo from which there is only one resolution possible. His body arches, his breathing rapid, his rigidity straining to burst forth as the master forces the drumbeat faster and louder. He only hears the drums now - the melody is gradually lost in the furor of the beat hammering at his senses. The master knows, he understands. I am attuned. I taste the impending flood, I thrill to the enormity between my lips, I know what chord to strike next. I feel the swelling of his pulsing prostate that is frantic to perform its solo aria at my direction. And when I choose, I bring my organ to full sforzando, fingers flying, lips pressuring precisely for that perfect harmony of pain and pleasure that I understand so well.

He fills my mouth with his essence, strung pearls of honey more precious to me than the most enthusiastic applause of a fancied audience, because I know that he has taken that perilous journey to the brink of death and will momentarily return to me for my kisses, his body quaking still as gravity again becomes dominant.

I know. I understand. I am a man who loves other men.

My life thus consists not only of my own orgasms,

159

supreme as they are, but my partners' orgasms as well. There are times when his orgasm is more satisfying than my own, when I can transport his life to that other plane, can feel vicariously the soaring, searing synergism of cock and balls and butt so like my own but different. And for that reason I must practice my skill as a master, always in training, always learning the nuances of response peculiar to the various "hims" who come my way. That is my challenge in life.

I have a grim competitor. A deadly virus, a clump of inanimate nucleic acids that threatens to steal my life's blood, my lovers, and my own immortality. "It" creeps into the most secret cells and disrupts them, converts them into its own slaves, plays its own dirges with a virtuosity worthy of a master. But it is a thief with skull and crossbones etched on its multiple facets, and it must be contained in a prison that I construct. It is a challenge to my orgasmic expertise, but I will defeat it because it has a fatal weakness - it does not love men.

I have mapped out a strategy for dealing with this interloper, this contorter of perfection, this grotesque monster who would deprive me of my orgasms so necessary for life. It will be banished by restricting its access to me and my lovers, and only I have the prowess to keep it trapped in its hideous cage. As with the demogogic gods of yore, it requires virgins to satisfy its voracious appetite. Only I can prevent its surges into virgin cells so necessary for its unspeakable existence. Only I can shield those precious virgins from the devastating horde of "its", and I can accomplish this feat because I am a master of orgasms.

No longer will my sperm kiss the rectal cells of my lovers, nor will theirs mine, I have ordained. I have always guarded and treasured my seed and the seed of my lovers, but now those mechanisms are to be strengthened. I must also restrict the internalization of that seed, so sweet, so satisfying, previously the very symbol of our love. The visual must be upgraded, a light show panoply to substitute for satiation of the taste buds. And I as a master of my art must provoke new appreciation for the tactile as well as the verbal aspects which were secondary in previous communications with my lovers.

My new approach as I move from orgasm to orgasm is to stimulate even further my lover's fantasies, which also potentiates my own. The rich and vital essence of masculinity is even more precious than before, sequestered in the warm nest, protected from enemies and even temperature changes. As we bring each other to life in order to experience that overwhelming near-death, we speak of the beauty we experience, we gaze upon each other's bodies and countenances, our hands busy with the unspoken language only men understand. Sometimes I use a surrogate cock that, I must admit, can work miracles even my own cannot. Our eyes lock as our bodies meet, and I show him the rigid evidence of my adoration even as his body is filled. My hands have become even more skillful in manipulating his prick, teasing the tender underside, my thumb riding over his apex lubricated with his inner oils. He tenses and strains, his facial features revealing his innermost thoughts and his eyes reading mine. As a special treat I stoop to lap the long, tendinous shaft but preserving the head for special attention. I sometimes treasure the fine hairs on his balls that decorate those little factories of his finest product. Only a man can produce such a product, and only a man can appreciate a "product" as a quintessential quality of life unique to a lover.

And when he can wait no longer, when I have brought his body's demands to their inevitable pinnacle, I return to the fountainhead with rotating strokes of my digital baton and feel it swell and pulsate, preparing for its crucial performance. It must wait until I concur, because

I am the master. Secretly I want it as much as he, and I do not prolong the perch on the precipice unless it pleases both of us.

When at last I perform that final magic, that *coup de grace* that sets him reeling and pitching on his flight to temporal death, I watch the cascade of purity and vitality gush from that phallic fountain accompanied by his cries of anguish and joy, each spurt, each drop perfection unsullied, straight from his boiling cauldrons so recently worshipped. Sometimes I direct his juices over me to welcome the hot potency on my feverish skin, and my senses reel almost as much as his as we traverse that weightless flight of orgasm together.

We have outwitted "the thing". We have shared a deathless moment of orgasm without giving up a victim, a virgin for it's voracious appetite. It is within our power to relegate it to the sewers or trap it inside condoms to die at length for need of a host. It will not come between us, two men who understand, who share innermost secrets without hesitation.

Even now I feel his hands on me, anxious for another moment of masculine ecstasy, another flight into the familiar but still unknown. And I give myself over to his supplication, already feeling the augmentation of my latent lust, the stirring that only another man can produce.

I move from orgasm to orgasm.

THE END

OTHER TITLES AVAILABLE
DIRECTLY FROM GLB PUBLISHERS

GAY/LESBIAN FICTION/POETRY

The Bunny Book   Novel by
John D'Hondt. The bunny mystique and
AIDS in a feminist setting.
288 pages   Paperback $11.95   _____

A Breviary Of Torment   Poems by
Thomas Cashet. Expressions of our love-
hate relationship with torture.
128 pages   Paperback $13.95
              Clothbound $28.95   _____

The Devil In Men's Dreams   Short
stories by **Tom Scott**. Gay men's
tales—but the devil made me do it.
246 pages   Paperback $11.95   _____

Good Night, Paul   Poems by
Robert Peters. Poems to a lover—"rapt,
comic, wry, and ebullient" for all lovers.
96 pages   Paperback $ 8.95   _____

*Snapshots For A Serial Killer: A Fiction
and a Play*, by **Robert Peters**. "A startling
and graphic monologue about violence..."
125 pages   Paperback $10.95   _____

SUB-TOTAL   _____

Add $2.00 per book for shipping: _____

TOTAL THIS PAGE   _____
(Turn the page for MORE new titles)

Check or money order to:

GLB Publishers

PO Box 78212   San Francisco, CA 94107